The Island of the Children

Morgan's Knot – A Serial Fantasy
Episode II

By

Eric T. Stiller, Jr.

The Island of the Children
Morgan's Knot – A Serial Fantasy
Episode II

A blazing smudge of liquid orange splattered firelight across the indigo water as the sun melted into the Pacific. Roger Johnson sat on the aft deck of his new yacht, the Tigger Too, watching his children, Todd and Sandy, fishing off the stern. They were anchored in a small isolated cove near the Bahia de San Quintin for the night, on their first run down the Mexican coast. His latest screenplay earned him a small fortune and the new boat was a reward to himself. It was one of the fastest racers on the water and comfortably accommodated six in the luxurious cabin below decks.

His wife, Peggy, was cleaning up the dishes in the galley and popped out of the hatch, "Like a beer?"

"Sure," replied Roger with a broad smile. He felt like the Cheshire Cat and thought to himself, *"Life is good."*

Peggy brought an icy bottle of Olympia to her husband, gave him a hug, and disappeared into the galley.

"Any bites?" He called to his children.

Todd turned and smiled, "Nothing yet, but I know they're down there!"

"You'll get one."

His daughter, Sandy, turned to her father, "Hey Dad, do you see that boat out there? It sure is coming fast!"

Roger gazed out through the mouth of the little cove. She was right, a boat was running wide open into the bay straight out of the last blazing wash of the sun. There were no running lights on the approaching craft and, as he watched, the hairs on the back of his neck began to prickle and a bead of cold sweat trickled down his cheek.

The boat turned hard at the last moment and settled next to the Tigger2. The driver, wearing a brightly colored Hawaiian shirt and sunglasses over a three-day growth of stubble, called out in a heavy Spanish accent, "Hey, mind if we anchor on the other side of the cove?"

Roger stood up, waved at the man standing at the wheel of the mystery boat, and called, "No, we don't mind."

The pilot of the other boat gunned the engines and smiled, "Great! Hope we're not disturbing you."

"Not at all."

"Have you seen any other boats this evening?"

"No, we're here alone," yelled Roger.

The boat drifted closer to the Tigger2 and several other men appeared on the deck brandishing small machine guns.

The children dropped their fishing rods and ran to their father.

The pilot of the other boat called out, "We'll be boarding you. Do not resist or we'll shoot los ninos!"

Three men from the second boat jumped aboard and hustled Roger and his children below decks.

"We'll be taking your kids with us and you'll take my comrades where they ask to go or you'll never see them again!"

Roger had no weapons on board and knew that he was no match for these muscular young men. There was no defense. A voice called down through the hatch, "His tanks are full."

One of the men held a gun on Roger and Peggy, while the other two carried the screaming children up the ladder, tossed them on the other boat and down to the cabin below, where they were bound and gagged. The captain chuckled to one of the other men, "We can't harm the children. It's the pirate's code. We'll leave them on the island and meet you at the rendezvous."

One of the pirates returned to the Tigger2 and said, "Let's get moving."

The second boat headed west as the Tigger2 turned north.

Chapter Two

Morgan's Knot buzzed with activity since the battle on the snowy peaks, Ester's rescue, and the introduction of Alius' father, who vanished with his daughter into the caverns inside the mountain for more than a week before reappearing at the observatory with four very large men, dressed in leather uniforms, to propose a conference of the elders from both sides of the island.

The councils from North and South met for days and there were rumors that the negotiations had been contentious at best, but representatives from each side were determined to mend the cleavage that separated their families for centuries.

The tunnel through the south side of the mountain was enlarged to accommodate vehicles and workers from both groups joined to construct a narrow road up a series of switchbacks from the base to the entrance.

Mandor and his men brought supplies to help rebuild the village and mechanics to get the two damaged trawlers running. Families, estranged for generations, began to discover each other and Elsie and Alius' great aunt, Shannon, were tracing family histories through hundreds of years. One of their first discoveries was that they were distant cousins, which explained Adrian and Alius' abilities as *seers*.

Nanchez and Ponte spent every day working together on the Crystals and the vectors. As Keepers of the Powers, they discovered that each had approached their science with unique needs and expectations and, consequently, different results. One was learning from the other and, as they merged their knowledge, they realized that both found secrets the other had missed.

Adrian thought they made quite a contrasting pair, Nanchez, a pale gruff giant with a mop of white hair, looming over Ponte, who was very short, extremely rotund, and shiny bald on top with thick tuffs of hair clinging around his ears and the collar of his bright green coat. The intensity of their interaction conjured the notion that they were two little kids who discovered their mutual love of the same intellectual game.

Jofre and the other Masters joined George, Dr. Stevens, Travis, and several elders almost every day to tour each side of the island and to work on merging their assets and efforts. Tall blond people joined in working the fields and tanned southerners toured the catacombs to begin learning about the technologies that allowed the Northerners to prosper through these many years.

Adrian and Alius were becoming fast friends, as they worked together on the Book of Wisdoms almost every day. Nanchez and Ponte, constantly seeking information or clarification of their theories, peppered them with questions for hours on end.

After a session at Ponte's table, George arrived to retrieve Adrian for dinner. As the trolley bumped through the gate and turned south on the path, the young *seer* searched to find a tactful way to ask his uncle about the search for his missing parents. He tried not to pester George and realized that things were changing for both sides at an incredible rate. Still, he felt certain they were alive but their survival might depend on beginning the journey as soon as possible.

"Have you given any thought to beginning our search?" Adrian asked with quiet hesitation.

"As a matter of fact, I have," replied George. His brow furrowed pensively. "The problem is that everyone is so busy trying to learn about our new friends and how to use the best of both worlds to merge our societies back together again. All of the adults are working day and night, so it might be hard to pull anyone away to crew the trawler for our journey."

Adrian pondered the dilemma with quiet resignation until he had an inspiration, "Why couldn't we use the children who rescued Ester? We proved that we're all capable of handling responsibilities beyond any adult's expectations and I'd be willing to bet every one of them would volunteer for this expedition."

George turned with a broad smile, "You might be on to something there. My only hesitation is that it might be a dangerous journey and their parents might not approve."

"We'll never know unless we ask."

"Okay. You get your friends together and propose your plan. If their parents will allow them to go, I think we can begin preparing."

Adrian was overwhelmed with a rush of excitement, knowing that he could convince the other children and they, in turn, could persuade their parents, "Well then, I guess I should ask the first parent. Would you allow Molly and Megan to go?"

George grimaced, "I don't think that decision is up to me. We'll have to persuade Elsie."

"Do I have your permission to ask the girls?"

"Yes…but you know your Aunt Elsie's not going to like this idea. No, she's not going to like this at all."

"I'm sure Molly and Megan will convince her."

Adrian found it hard to contain his excitement during dinner and Elsie commented on the steadfast smile plastered across his face. "You seem unusually chipper this evening."

The boy blushed and ducked his head, "Oh, it's just seeing everything changing so fast."

"It is amazing," said George, deflecting the inquiry. "I was totally astonished at the sophistication of their engineering. Every system in that entire complex rivals the very latest cutting edge work being done in the real world, the fit and finish is astonishing."

Elsie interrupted, "Would anyone like some desert?"

After dinner, Elsie and George went to the barn to feed the animals and the children were left to wash the dishes. Adrian was scrubbing, Molly drying, and Megan was putting everything away. Adrian walked to the back door, dripping soapsuds across the floor, to make sure that his aunt and uncle were in the barn and then turned back to the girls, "I've convinced your father to begin the search for my parents but there's a problem. The adults are all busy with the work that's being done around the island, so I proposed that we use our friends to crew the trawler. Your Dad thought it was a good idea, so I asked him if you two could go and he said that you'd have to win your Mother's approval. Do you want to go?"

Both girls broke into giggles. Molly couldn't contain the squeals erupting from somewhere behind her nose, so Adrian clamped his hand over her mouth. "Sshhhh! Your mom will hear you!"

"I'm sorry, I'm just excited."

"Do you think you can talk her into going along with our plan?"

"I know we can!" said Megan. "Just let us work on her for a couple of days."

"Great! We can talk with Morgan, Josh, Ian, and Kelly tomorrow."

John and Sara awoke to the snarl of a boat's engines humming in the distance and moving closer.

It had been weeks since their sloop, The Sparrow, was pulverized in the hurricane and they could only hope that a ship or yacht might happen by the island. Wood for a bonfire was stacked and kindling ready for the match...or spark in this case.

From the tree house, constructed in a huge sprawling banyan tree behind the dunes above the beach, they could see a sleek speedboat approaching. It slowed and idled to within a few yards of the beach.

The engines rumbled quietly while two men waded through the surf, carrying wrapped bundles over their shoulders. They set the two packages on the beach and snatched off the coverings to reveal two children. Sara grabbed John and gasped, "They're kids..."

The men turned and waded back out to their boat, throttled the engines, and headed back out to sea. The children jumped around the beach screaming and waving desperately.

Before they could drop the rope ladder, a cluster of small nearly naked people with ashen gray skin rushed from the bush. They swarmed down the beach, gathered the two children, and vanished into the jungle.

Adrian's parents looked at each other bewildered, scrambled down from the tree house, and ran to the place where the children disappeared. A school of small footprints traced away into the jungle past a cross and crescent that Sara constructed on the sand with colored pebbles, in case an airplane happened by, but the trail faded after a few yards in the dense undergrowth.

"Well, now we know who's been leaving our gourmet meals!" said Sara. Each morning, they found woven plates of fish or meat, a wonderful mash of cooked breadfruit, occasionally, something akin to real bread, and an assortment of fruits beneath the tree house. Try as they might, they had never been able to catch whoever was leaving the gifts.

"I think we ought to explore a bit more of this island. We've only seen parts of it and, if there are other people living here, there has to be a sign of their activity somewhere. We should be able to find them."

"Let's start up on the ridge. At least we'll have a bird's eye view," said John.

"Right you are, let's go," replied Sara.

They gathered materials they found in the forest and along the beach to construct the tree house, the jungle provided ample fruits and nuts, and they found crabs and mussels around rocky outcrops pounded by the surf. The gifts of food started to appear in the gnarly roots beneath their temporary home a few days after they arrived. They investigated parts of the island and found animal trails tracing through the jungle but no evidence of other people living on the island, other than a single pair of small footprints that led to and from the brush to the point where the platters rested on the rocks around the fire pit each morning.

When they returned to the tree house, they found two plates of nuts, fruits, and chunks of boiled crab wrapped in a small tortilla. Although they were anxious to start their exploration to find some trace of those two children, they sat down and ate the food that had been offered. Sara stood to gather some supplies and felt faint. She looked down as John fell over on the sand and collapsed beside him.

Josh, Ian, Morgan, and Kelly jumped out of the wagon and ran across the yard. Adrian noticed that Kelly was slow to catch up and hid behind the other children, "Hi! What have you learned?"

"Our parents will let us go, if at least one other adult goes along…well, all of us except Kelly. My parents think she's too young for this journey but we're still working on them," said Ian.

"I'm sorry Kelly," said Adrian, crouching to share a hug. "We all know that you're more than capable, you've already proved yourself. Maybe we can convince them to let you come along."

"Maybe," whispered Kelly. She was staring at the ground and Adrian could feel her disappointment.

"I'll talk to George when he gets back from the village," said Adrian. "He's checking with Travis about the trawler. Elsie has reluctantly agreed to allow Molly and Megan to go along."

Brandy bounded up the path, "I hear you're planning another adventure and I want to go too. You'll need some animal help!"

Adrian bent down to pet the Irish setter. "Have you ever been on a boat?"

"Well, no…but I don't see any reason why I couldn't adapt and besides, who knows what you'll run into when you finally reach dry ground again. I could be useful."

"If you go, then Tic will want to go too."

"Great!"

Adrian turned to the other children, who were all smiling, "What do you think?"

Morgan smiled and reached out to pet Brandy, "I think that you couldn't have replaced the black diamond and we couldn't have retrieved Ester without Tic and Brandy's help."

"You're right."

Brandy barked, "Great! I'll tell Tic!" and ran out the gate, charging up the path to the north.

Travis took off his hat and brushed the perspiration from his brow, "I don't know about one adult and a crew of kids with no experience on the water. I just don't feel right letting you take the risk."

"John and Sara are out there somewhere and I've promised Adrian that we'd go look for them at the first opportunity. After all that he's done for us, I can't let him down. Besides, these children have already proven themselves under battle conditions, I think that they can do this."

"I'll tell you what…I've been getting to know Demetre, the *other's* port master, and I'm beginning to have great respect for his mechanical skills and his knowledge of the water. What would you think if I went with you? I'm sure he can handle things here while we're gone and his guys know their stuff."

"I'd love to have you along. You know far more about these boats and the ocean than I ever will but I'd hate to pull you away."

"It's been a long time since I took a voyage, I'm rather looking forward to it," said Travis with a broad smile.

"Right then. It's settled. I'll get back to you tonight after I find out what the other parents have decided about our crew. I'm off to Ponte's. Anything that you need from him?"

"No, we're in good shape here. All of the trawlers are running again and the village is almost completely repaired. Call me on the *messenger* later."

They shook hands and George hopped into the trolley and drove out of the village to the path that turned north to the observatory.

———————

Nanchez was just leaving and greeted George with a pat of his giant hand that forced the old farmer to take a step to maintain his balance. "Hello! How are ya'?" He was not a small man but he felt like a midget next to the enormous Keeper.

Ponte laughed as he led George into the parlor, "He's different!"

"That he is. How's the work coming with The Crystals?"

"He knows as much as I do about how they work but we know different things. It's rather fascinating really. I've studied these powers and vectors for decades and there have always been questions…areas that I just couldn't figure out. He has the answers that I've been looking for and I have the solutions that he's been seeking. So, we're both learning."

"The reason that I've come to see you is that Adrian is anxious to begin searching for his parents and I've agreed to take him on one of the trawlers. Travis has decided that if anyone is going, he's going. I guess he doesn't trust me with his precious boat but I certainly bow to his experience. Considering how busy all of the adults have been, Adrian came up with the idea of asking his friends to crew and they're talking with their parents. I feel fairly confident in their abilities, after all they did to rescue Ester."

"They'll make a fine crew. What they don't know, they'll learn," said Ponte. He was quiet for a moment, the eyes behind his little glasses focused on something across the cluttered parlor. George could see the wheels turning inside his head. Finally, he said, "You know, this might be a terrific opportunity to learn about another Crystal, if, indeed, that is where his parents landed, one that has, perhaps, never been revealed by another human being. I'm going too!"

George looked down at the broad smile on the little man's face, "How could I say no to an offer like that?"

"You can't. Besides, Nanchez confirmed my assumption that the vectors that we've been using for all these many years aren't confined to this island. They extend out across the globe and all of the other Crystals are loosely connected in something like a web of energy. I'm confident that Ester and Nanchez can handle the vectors while I'm gone. Alius is certainly capable of translating from the Book of Wisdoms and formal classes don't start for more than two months."

Ponte wandered back to the table, where Adrian and Alius had been working on the Book and picked up a round instrument that was about the size of a soccer ball, "This is something that Nanchez loaned me. I guess the only way to describe its function is that it is something like a vector radio. It allows the user to utilize the vectors for transmitting voice and data from one place to another, like the system we have on this island…only globally, and it also provides a means to track those vectors and The Crystals anyplace in the world. He was wise enough to integrate channels for both the light and the dark energies, so this might be useful in our search."

George took the instrument from the Professor and examined it. It was very heavy. Crystals glowed around a small screen inset in a textured surface with knobs, dials, and gauges above and below. A strange spiral antenna grew out of the top of the sphere. In spite of his engineering degree, George was bewildered by the instrument and handed it back to the expert, "I'll leave the science in your hands but I'd be honored to have you accompany us on our trip."

Tic stood from his nap on the back of the sofa, jumped to the floor, and slowly wandered over to the two men. Ponte leaned over to pick him up.

The old cat rubbed his head under the Professor's chin, "Of course you know that I'll be going along too. You people would never have been successful, in your more recent quests, without the help of the animals on the island and, when you get to where you are going, you'll need my talents again."

George and Ponte laughed and agreed.

"Brandy's going too."

"How do you know that?" asked Ponte.

"He came by this morning. All of the children are going, except Kelly, and he made the children promise that he could go too."

George smiled, "Now we have a crew."

Chapter Three

The parents stood huddled together on the docks waving as the old trawler, Jasmine, idled out of the little cove into a ferocious wind howling from the north, scraping clouds of foam from the crests of churning whitecaps. A flock of seagulls fell in behind the fishing boat, swooping around the stern and cawing loudly. Her hold was laden with crates of food and supplies in addition to the many cases of mysterious equipment hauled aboard from the red trolley.

Alius had been raised to place her duty before her own desires and accepted the necessity of one *seer* remaining on the island but she was disappointed to be left behind. She hugged each of her new friends in turn and Adrian last, "You're like a brother to me and I treasure our friendship. Do what you must but come back alive."

At the last minute, Ian and Kelly's parents relented, allowing Kelly to accompany the older children on this latest adventure. Sheridan Keelty clutched her daughter until the very last moment and looked up into George's eyes, "You must promise to bring them all back safely."

"I promise," he vowed. "I'll care for them as if they were my own but I also have great confidence in each of them, including Kelly. They proved themselves on the mountain a few weeks ago."

All of the children wrapped Kelly in a bear hug and Adrian decided that her wonderful smile was reason enough to have her along. He glanced up to see a large black raven diving low over the little harbor, its black feathers glistening in the early morning sun as it closed on the trawler with long slow sweeps of massive wings. Magnus, the eagle, swooped down from the bluffs above the crescent beach with a piercing screech, diving hard with talons extended to escort the immense intruder out to sea.

The young *seer* looked down at Kelly's smile as she waved good-bye to the crowd on the dock, "That was weird."

"That bird?"

"Yes, and Magnus showing up to chase him away."

"I've never seen a black bird that big on the island," said Kelly.

"I've only seen them once or twice and I always get a bad feeling. Maybe it's just superstition or something…"

"I don't believe in superstition but I do believe in the things that you…sense…is that the right word?"

"Yes…I've never really thought about it," smiled Adrian.

"Well, you should."

A flutter of wings interrupted, as Magnus landed on the rail. The huge bird leaned forward to rub his beak up and down Adrian's nose then cocked his head, "Mind if I join you? I've never been to the tropics and, besides, you might need reconnaissance."

Spot and Dusty vowed that their relatives would guide the trawler safely to their destination and escorted them for the first leg of the voyage, handing the old ship over to their cousins, who led or followed them for days before passing them over to another pair of dolphins.

Ponte produced books, charts, boxes full of instruments, and enough work to keep the children occupied for most of each day.

"This is supposed to be an adventure," whined Molly, "not a floating schoolhouse."

"What better place to transform concept and theory into practical applications?" replied the Professor, who wore a turquoise bow tie and wool vest. "This is where you get to see the results of the things that you're learning immediately."

"We were kinda hoping for a little time to kick back for a cruise," added Megan.

"Small chance of that," griped Molly.

Ponte chuckled and gathered his students on the deck for their first lesson with an ancient sextant, charts, a wonderful clock and an old brass compass in a wooden box spread across a table on the aft deck, "Ancient mariners traveled the world over and, through the ages, the biggest challenge was in knowing where they were located on the globe. The earliest sailors used the sun and the stars to guide their voyages and that process continues to this day. These are the instruments that will allow us to set a course to our destination."

"We have a very precise clock set to Greenwich Mean Time. You've all learned about longitude and latitude, the invisible lines that divide the globe into 360 degrees east and west, north and south. If we were to project those lines into space and, if we were to pretend that all the stars lie on a glass globe that surrounds the earth, then we could divide the heavens by that grid."

He pulled the sextant from its case, "This is called a sextant. It is a very precise instrument that allows us to measure the angle from the sun or a star to the horizon. If we were to take readings and we knew the exact time and direction, we could consult the nautical almanac to find our precise location. Using a compass and the angles of rise, as well as north and south, provides enough information to know where you are."

"I know this sounds complicated but, in a few days, each of you will begin to understand the process. I realize that Kelly has not been introduced to geometry yet, so I would ask each of you to help her learn the method of triangulation. We'll all work on this together and then we'll form teams of two to take the readings. This must be done seven times each day."

Ponte unrolled a large chart, "This is a nautical chart. It shows the landmasses and the depth of the water, which is particularly useful near the coasts. As you can see, there are curved lines graphing the depths. These run concurrently to indicate shallow areas and deeper channels. We wouldn't want to run aground!"

"As you learn to find our location, we'll transfer that information to these charts to chronicle our progress. Are there any questions?"

Kelly raised her hand, "What's triangulation? It sounds like strangulation!"

Ian brushed his hand across his throat, "It's not like strangulation at all!" Everyone laughed. "We'll teach you, it isn't hard. Basically, it means that, if you added the inside angles of any triangle, they would always equal one hundred and eighty degrees. If you know two angles of a triangle, then you can figure out the third angle. Does that make sense?"

Kelly looked a little bit bewildered, "Well, sort of…?"

Adrian piped in, "I've sailed with my parents and I've used a sextant a few times with my dad. I understand the principles and I'd be happy to have Kelly as my partner."

Kelly smiled her biggest smile and moved to sit next to Adrian. Brandy, just beginning to find his sea legs, slid awkwardly across the deck to plop next to Kelly. He reached up and gave her a big lick. Tic sauntered across the chart, rolled out on the table, and settled down for a little nap.

Josh asked, "Why can't we just use the radar and instruments on the boat?"

"Because this is your chance to master a precise method of establishing your location and, in the process, you will apply mathematical formulas, establish a working knowledge of the heavens, and establish a profound appreciation for nautical charts. A small effort for a large reward, considering it might well save our lives," said the old man kindly. "Is that reason enough?"

"Yes, sir."

Over the next few days, they practiced each step in the procedure and, soon, each team was routinely providing precise information to add to the charts. The Professor taught them to find the planets and the constellations and, each evening, recounted stories of the meanings and significance attributed to the stars and constellations by the ancients.

Travis provided a wooden box with a piece of glass in the bottom that they lowered over the side for a clear view of reefs and fish swimming in shallow waters. All of the children were fascinated by the hidden and mysterious wonderland that surrounded Morgan's Knot and stretched around the globe.

They fished along the way and it wasn't long before the students were able to name each fish caught. Brandy watched every cast into the sea with great expectation and pranced around the deck each time a line went taut. Tic, on the other hand, was perfectly content to nap until the fish had been cleaned before barging in to demand scraps for a snack.

Magnus, a master fisherman, would soar off to scout the course and check the winds each morning and always returned with a prize for his breakfast. He settled on the transom to devour a shiny golden mackerel, "Why anyone would want to char something so fresh and delicious is beyond me."

Everyone joined in cooking meals and cleaning up the galley and they were learning to become self-sufficient yet an integral part of the team. Travis made each child pilot the craft, read the wind and the waves, and learn to understand the mechanical workings of the old trawler. When there was a problem with one of the systems, he would guide the children to trace down the glitch and find a solution. Two man teams were responsible for manning each watch, rotating through two-hour shifts and altering schedules every few days, which allowed time for everyone to rest.

George brought along several volumes of history and geography and there were lessons each afternoon on the people who first ventured into the unknown to explore and inhabit the Caribbean and Central and South America. Then they delved into violent invasions by the Spanish, English, Dutch, and the Portuguese, which led to the demise of ancient civilizations, sophisticated societies rich in culture, art, medicine, astronomy, and architecture. The invaders seized, not only gold and gems, but great tracts of land for cotton, sugar cane, coffee, and cocoa, which fanned the markets for slaves who were kidnapped, crammed into the bellies of trading ships in Africa, and dispatched to plantations in the new world.

At one session, Adrian raised his hand, "I have a question. I've noticed the even sided cross and crescent moon with the tiny star on the spinnaker on my parent's boat, in the Book of Wisdoms, and in various places on Morgan's Knot. I was wondering about its significance?"

George smiled, "In contemporary times, most crosses have become the recognized symbol of Christianity. The even sided cross was adopted as the universal icon for the Eastern Orthodox Church and the crescent, a symbol of Islam and other Eastern Religions, and the six pointed star for Judaism."

"Historically, each was used by various societies around the world for thousands of years preceding any religious connotation. Originally, the cross, enclosed in the crescent, was revered as the mark of the balance of mankind within nature, between man and woman, between earth and sky, fire and water, and all the opposing forces that mankind faced in the quest for survival and progress. The star represents a guard to regulate the equilibrium of the energies."

"In ancient times, women were held in high esteem. They were the members of society who brought life into the world and their fertility was viewed as sacred. Women were certainly as well educated as men and their views and opinions played a vital role in governing and the social order. We continue that belief to this day," he laughed, "although I've sometimes suspect that the women in our midst really do control our little society without much consideration of the male point of view, so any imbalance is certainly tilted in their favor. Our mathematical system uses this cross to indicate addition and, if you turn it on its side, multiplication. Of course, it was also the symbol for the balance between the positive and negative forces of The Crystals."

Morgan smirked, "Nice to have the social order of our little society clarified!"

"I always thought you girls were kinda pushy," laughed Josh.

Adrian interrupted, "So it's not necessarily a religious symbol in its use by those who live by the powers of The Crystals?"

George grinned, "We use the symbol in recognition of The Balance, so in the traditional sense, no, it's not necessarily religious...but, on the other hand, it is so much more. I would not suggest that I know the answers to the religious questions that have been raised by every generation of every faith in every society over the course of history. Those are beliefs that each of you must resolve for yourselves but we must realize that, in addition to our personal convictions, we are the stewards of The Balance. Every religious text has directives about Man living in harmony with nature and caring for the world around us. Man certainly didn't invent these Crystals or the powers that we work so hard to perpetuate and protect."

A contemplative quiet lasted for several long moments, before George finally said, "Perhaps we should view the cross and the crescent as the symbols for the way things should be in our world and our dedication to maintaining and improving the conditions of life for every living creature. I think that whatever God you believe in would be pleased with that commitment."

The days passed quickly and there was little time for boredom with chores, maintenance, and studies. Travis and George consulted over the charts on the map table behind the bridge and decided to follow along the eastern route around Cuba to Jamaica. Montego Bay provided enough points of interest to divert the pent-up energies of the children and an inviting port to refuel and replenish their supplies of water and food before diving southwest to the Panama Canal.

The sun was setting over the cliffs to the west and the oranges and yellows of the evening sky glittered across gentle ripples striping the water as they entered the bay. Travis guided the old trawler to a wooden dock at the far end of the quay, where a slender black boy with a mane of curly black ringlets was waiting.

"Bumpers out!" cried Morgan from the bridge, gently gunning the engines in reverse. Kelly, Josh, and Ian pushed bumpers over the starboard side as the stern glided to rest beside the pilings under the dock. Molly and Megan threw lines from the bow and stern and the lad tied them off to cleats on the wooden gangplank.

"Welcome to Montego Bay," cried the boy, as the children clamored onto the pier. "You have many children!" He stopped and stared, "And a red dog, a huge cat, and…a giant bird?"

Brandy barked, Magnus squawked loudly, and all the children laughed.

Travis replied, "Thank you, it's been a long trip but it's good to have an energetic crew. Could we get some fuel and fresh water?"

"Sure, Mon. I can take care of that for you." The boy's smile was infectious and the melodic flow of his accent made a joyous song of every sentence that escaped his mouth, "You'll be wanting to re-supply your food too?"

"Yes, we will. Is there a grocery on the wharf?" inquired George.

"Sure, Mon. Just up the way here," he said, pointing to a small shack with a sign that said 'FOOD' "or you can go down to the tourist stores at the other end."

Adrian stooped to coil a line and the boy reached out to shake his hand, "My name is Sammy."

The young *seer* shook hands with the dockhand, who might have been a year older than Adrian, and noticed that he wore a ring with a deep blue stone. A perfect cross, surrounded by a slender crescent moon, shimmered like pearls and stood in relief above the face of the gem. "Nice to meet you. My name is Adrian."

"You're a special one. I can tell. Welcome to Jamaica. It is a magical place."

Adrian blushed, staring at the boy inquisitively, "I seem to have a habit of finding magical places."

"That does not surprise me. You'll be wanting to go for a visit to the market."

"The market?"

"Yes, it's not far from here. The stalls will be open in the morning. You and your friends should go for a visit. They sell all sorts of things there and it is a special place. You never know who you might meet or what you might find. It is different every day."

"Well, I don't know how long we'll be here."

"You should make time to visit the market. Believe me, I know."

Ponte was standing on the deck, listening to the conversation. He looked at the boy with intense interest, "That's an interesting ring you're wearing."

"Ah, it belonged to my father and his father before him. We believe that it symbolizes magic in its most perfect form."

"I've seen that mark before. What does it mean?"

"Jamaica is a magical island. We believe that it represents the powers of a mysterious ancient people who visited the island for a short time. When they departed, they left some of the magic here. It is something that we feel but do not control."

"That's an interesting story. Why would the children enjoy the market?" inquired Ponte.

"Ah, there are special people there. It is more than a place to buy and sell. Beneath the commerce, it is like a human newspaper spreading news and information through the people and our elders gather there to dispense wisdom and justice. I sense that this young man might find it interesting. It is not far, perhaps a fifteen or twenty minute walk or you could take a taxi."

"Well, we'll be spending the night, so we'll think about it. I'm sure the children would love some real food. Is there a restaurant that serves local cuisine?"

"Yes, Mon, just up the quay, there are restaurants that serve American food but if you want Jamaican food, turn to the right and go two blocks. It's called Mona's and she is a wonderful cook. You will enjoy your meal."

"Thank you. We'll take your suggestion. Is it alright if we leave the boat here?"

"Sure, Mon. I'll keep an eye on her."

Adrian and Ponte exchanged a look, as the young *seer* pushed and Sammy pulled the Professor's considerable girth onto the dock. Travis paid the boy for the fuel and water and wandered after the rest of the crew to the grocery.

They bought staples and treats and returned to stow the food in the lockers on the boat. The girls all wanted to take a shower and George decided that they could all stand to be clean, so they took turns running back and forth to the shower stalls on the dock.

As twilight dwindled into darkness, they trooped up the wharf and turned to the right to find the restaurant that Sammy suggested. Mona met them at the door, "Welcome to Mona's! You look hungry, come in, come in!" She pushed several tables together to accommodate the crowd and brought giant platters of seafood, meats, and fresh vegetables to be shared by all. Everyone was fascinated with the breadfruit, which was served mashed like holiday potatoes. Morgan recounted the story of The Mutiny on the Bounty and the plants that were being transported back to Europe. The meal was wonderful and George, Ponte, and Travis enjoyed several beers.

Adrian pulled a chair next to Ponte and asked in hushed tones, "What do you make of our friend Sammy?"

"That was curious, wasn't it?"

"A bit close to home. I almost felt that he knew I was a *seer* but I didn't want to say anything."

"And rightly so. I see no reason why we shouldn't take a little stroll in the morning and see what the market has to offer, if you'd like?"

"I have to admit he sparked my curiosity. Do we have time?"

"Sure, we'll make time. Unless they're incredibly lucky, I would doubt your parents are going anywhere until we find them."

The boy was quiet for a moment, staring at the ring of foam in the Professor's glass of beer, "Do you think there are Crystals on this island?"

"I don't know and I have no idea about whether his story is just that, a story, or whether it has deeper meaning. He certainly picked you out of the group."

"Yes, he did. I wasn't sure about what was happening."

"You said the Golden Crystal showed you where the Crystals existed all over the globe. Did you happen to notice any in the Caribbean?"

"The last time I was in the Crystal, I was more interested in the west coast of Mexico and, if I remember correctly, I was about to pass out."

"Well, let's see what happens tomorrow," said Ponte, patting Adrian on the back. "As we've already proved, the Crystals work in mysterious ways."

They finished the last crumbs of desert and walked back to the Jasmine for the night. Reggae music blared from several small clubs along the streets above the wharf and the children danced across the dock to the old trawler.

After everyone settled down for the night, Ponte brought one of his cases up to the deck and settled down on the bench across the stern. He opened the clasps, lifted the lid, and removed a gray sphere with some difficulty. He turned several knobs and mashed two buttons. A soft whistling sound descended in tone and volume, as tiny crystals began to pulse across the surface of the gray ball.

Tic wandered over, "What is that machine? That sound is annoying and it makes me feel cold."

"Aye, there's a black crystal inside, along with an amber one. I'll be done in a minute."

The cat jumped onto the stern, "I'll just watch from over here."

The professor adjusted a strange antenna and the tone grew steady. He inspected the gauges and turned a dial, before leaning back to stare at two glowing dots on the tiny screen with a soft whistle. "They do have a pair of Crystals here!"

Adrian awoke the next morning to aromas wafting from the galley where Kelly and Josh were fixing breakfast and, in spite of the huge feast they shared the night before, he was famished.

They all gathered around the table in the cabin for eggs, bacon, fresh fruit, and muffins…and cold, fresh orange juice.

"This is so good," said Molly, through a mouthful of muffin. It's been too long since we had a meal that hadn't been frozen…or included fish!"

They all laughed. Ponte spoke, "Do we have time for a little excursion before we head out again?"

George and Travis looked at each other, "Sure, why not? What'd you have in mind?"

"Our friend Sammy had an interesting conversation with Adrian last night. He was wearing a beautiful ring with a perfect cross, surrounded by a crescent moon. He picked Adrian out of the group and said that he was a "special one." He also suggested that Adrian might find the market interesting and that it's only a short walk from here."

George looked at Adrian, "What did he say to you?"

"He said that Jamaica was a magical island, once inhabited by people who left some of their magic here before they disappeared. He also said that there were special people in the market and that I should take the time to explore it."

George pondered the thought, "I find it interesting that he picked you out of the group to relate that particular story. We have time for a little exploration. Let's take the man's advice and see what we find."

Morgan turned to the animals, "You guys think you can look after the Jasmine while we're gone?"

"Who's going to try to board a ship with a barking dog, snarling cat, and enormous eagle?" replied Tic.

"No one who has any brains," laughed Ponte.

The group set off through the maze of streets up the hills behind the opulent hotels near the water through neighborhoods that looked unchanged for years. Although aging and sometimes decrepit, the homes and storefronts were painted in vibrant colors and flowers bloomed in every open space. The melodic accent of the people on the street, as much musical rhythm as conversation, carried them along like a smooth wave on the water.

After a twenty minute walk, they passed through a narrow alley into the rough remnants of a huge open plaza filled with little stalls selling an endless variety of goods, including clothes and tie-die tee-shirts, trinkets, records, jewelry, perfumes, and piles of colorful fabrics, as well as local foods. It was certainly a shopper's paradise...colorful, noisy, and roiling with energy.

The children wandered in and out of one stall after another. Ponte, George, and Travis took turns herding them along. Kelly and Adrian stopped at a trinket shop covered with a yellow tarp and the smallest sailor was entranced by the jewelry made of tiny shells. Adrian asked George whether he could buy a little bracelet for Kelly and his uncle gave him some money.

Adrian paid the woman with the bright orange headscarf in the stall and helped put the little bracelet on her wrist. Kelly was so pleased she gave Adrian a big hug and flashed that wonderful smile, "Thank you, Adrian. I'll wear it forever!"

"You're welcome, now let's go find the rest of the kids."

Morgan and Molly were pawing though fabric in a stall across the way. "Aren't the colors incredible?" asked Morgan, as she held up a bolt of bright blue fabric. "My mother has been teaching me how to sew. I'd love to take her a present when we go back."

Travis walked up to the children and admired the fabric that Morgan was holding up. "That's a lovely color and the cloth is so sheer. It's beautiful."

"Could I buy a piece for my mother? I know that she'd love it."

"I bet we could swing that," said Travis with a smile. "How much do you need?"

"Oh, a few yards. I know she could make something beautiful with this."

Adrian pulled the corner of the fabric away from the bolt and held it up. It shimmered in the clear light.

An old man stood behind an ancient table sagging under the weight of the fabrics. He was small and wiry. His skin was very dark and he had a little white goatee and tiny pair of glasses sitting on the end of a broad nose. "That is a very special fabric. They say that it is the fabric of the kings and as fine as the feathers in a hummingbird's wings. It almost matches the color of your eyes." The old man was looking directly at Adrian.

"It is very beautiful," said Adrian, as Ponte wandered up to join the group.

Morgan handed the bolt of material to the old man, who proceeded to mark out three yards, then added an extra little bit to his measurement. He wore a pendant around his neck that swayed back and forth across his chest as he worked. It almost matched the color of the fabric. Adrian noticed that it was decorated with a perfect cross and a crescent moon that was exactly like the ring the dockhand, Sammy, had on his hand.

"That's an interesting pendant you're wearing," said Adrian.

The old man looked up from his work and stared over his tiny glasses, "We believe that Jamaica is a magical island. This is the symbol of an ancient people that lived here for a short time. We believe that it is the sign of the *seer*."

"What do you know of *seers*?"

"It is believed that *seers* were blessed with ability to read from the ancient texts, the books that held the answers to the questions of the ages. As the story goes, the magic books were handed down from one generation to the next. It was all started by a man named Protus."

"That's an interesting name. What else can you tell me?" asked Adrian. He felt Ponte standing at his side.

"I can tell you what I told a woman who shared this same conversation a couple of months ago. She had eyes the same color as yours," he stopped. "I told the beautiful lady that she would find more than she was looking for…and so will you."

"Tell me about the lady," said Adrian, his mind racing.

"She was with a large man with dark hair. They stopped in my stall and bought some of this same fabric. She had blond hair, like yours, and a marvelous smile. I never saw her again, but I believe that I will."

Adrian turned to Ponte, who wore the same knowing smile he had on his face when Adrian had first read from the Book of Wisdoms, "Are you a *seer*?"

"I would like to believe that I am but I have no way of proving it." Turning to Adrian, he said, "You, on the other hand, you are probably a *seer*."

"And why would you say that?"

"It's in your eyes. I know that look and I will tell you something else. You'll return here. I will see you again."

He wrapped the fabric in brown paper and handed it to Morgan. "There you go, pretty lady, I'm sure that your mother will appreciate it." Travis paid the man and joined the other children, who were wandering away.

The old man held out his hand and Adrian shook it, feeling a tingling in his fingers, a tiny electrical current flowing between them. It reminded him of the sensation that he had when he was standing before the giant Crystal. He felt the energy being drained from his body, withdrew his hand, and said quietly, "Thank you for your time."

"It is my pleasure and I look forward to seeing you again. It won't be long."

Adrian and Ponte turned and walked over to George, Travis, and the other children, who were discussing where to find a meal before they returned to the boat.

"That was an interesting conversation," remarked Ponte.

"I've heard the expression about the world being a small place. How could that man possibly know about *seers*, let alone that I am one?" wondered Adrian.

"I'm sure that we aren't the only people in the world who know about the powers of *seers*, but this encounter was more than chance. I'm not sure what to make of it but the fact that he came up with the name Protus is intriguing. I wonder whether Protus was a descendant of those original mariners who escaped Atlantis perhaps? That would explain the Inca and Mayan cultures and their predecessors and the appearance of pyramids thousands of miles from Egypt."

Adrian turned back to the old man with the pendant but the stall was bare.

Chapter Four

Safra stood alone at the center of the temple, his head tilted into a shimmering shaft of golden light rushing through a circular hole in the peak of the ceiling like a sword of luminescent gemstones. The fact that it fell straight down to illuminate a human heart, etched in a circle of jade inlaid at the center of a golden starburst with beams splayed out like radians of the equatorial sun in the smooth stones beneath his feet, marked the equinox. He turned his face to the sunlight and prayed for guidance from the Sun God, Thoth, as he had so many times before.

Ameridus, keeper of the codex (a complicated system for charting the movements of the stars and the planets through the thirteen layers of the universe), had been granted an audience, several days before, to discuss the impending alignment of the planets and the stars. He was most concerned about prophecies foretelling the end of the Mayan world.

According to the divinations, four jaguars supported the corners of a flat world and, when all of the planets lined up beneath the world tree in the sky, they would gobble up the fabric of the living world and all life would cease to exist.

"The signs are aligned in accordance with the ancient prophecies. There can be no doubt that these white devils, risen from the sea, fulfill the promise of our demise. The calendar predicts this precise moment in our history. I've confirmed the divinations in the texts, and, as a final affirmation, I entered the Crystal, which revealed an identical warning. The time has come."

The King's emissaries met with the pale people who came from the sea and relayed an alert that the white men from the ships with many sails were dressed for battle and demanding further concessions. The first group, bribed with baskets of gold and shiny stones, sailed away in their mighty ships, only to return in the past months with more vessels and a larger force. Safra was an old man, honored to have guided his people through fifty years of peace in one of the last enclaves of a once vast society, but he realized that these new invaders would not be satisfied with a few baskets of gold.

Today, Thoth was silent. Thoth's warm blessing fell on Safra's face yet he felt a chill run down his bony spine and he knew that no sacrifice, no prayers would change the movement in the heavens or the impending catastrophe.

He knelt down, his white robes gleaming white flames in the brilliant beam, and touched his forehead to the heart within the crescent in the circle of jade in the floor. His golden crown wrapped around his skull like a slender serpent and the sacred feathers of the quetzal, attached to the back of the coronet, fluttered in a cool but gentle breeze that flowed through the chamber.

A single tear rolled down his cheek, as he sat back on his haunches and faced the warm stream of sunlight. He touched the fingertips of each hand together lightly and raised his face to talk to his God, "I humbly seek your guidance, as I have so many times before. I fear that I have offended you, that I have failed my people, and I see no path that might lead us to your blessing for the texts describe the demise of our culture. I pray for some alternative, some salvation for my people," He paused, "your people, for I am only your most humble surrogate, your messenger, your servant..."

Safra waited for some response, some sign that might guide him, but there was only silence in the huge chamber, save the dejected thump of his heart's reluctant beat and the sound of his own breath. Slowly, the shaft of light withered, as an eclipse blocked the sun, and the sacred chamber turned cold and dark. The message had been delivered.

His old bones ached, as he rose and shuffled slowly to the secret entrance to the King's sanctuary. His daughter Nanu was waiting and wrapped her arm through his as she gazed into his tired eyes. They stood together at the top step of the pyramid, in silence, and surveyed the vast city.

Citizens moved about the metropolis, attending to their duties completely unaware of the impending cataclysm. Their ancestors devised systems that provided shelter from mighty storms, irrigation to compensate for droughts, a harmonious farming tradition that provided amply for the entire population, natural defenses against their enemies, and medicines that calmed fevers and saved thousands of lives, but there was no salvation from these invaders without the blessing and guidance of the gods.

A grand plaza stretched away from the pyramid, surrounding a giant pool reflecting the jungle climbing great mountain peaks surrounding the metropolis. They had shared many religious ceremonies and festivals on this step, far above the masses that assembled to receive the Emperor's blessing. This would be the first major event in the history of his people that he would not share with them before it occurred. The future of the heritage and the knowledge depended on secrecy.

"I have failed my people, although I do not blame our ancestor's decision to abandon the sacrifices, in spite of our banishment from the old tribe. Thoth approved of our allegiance to the Balance," sighed Safra. "Soon, this vast city will empty and our society will cease to exist. It is time for the unthinkable. We must send the sacred texts to a place where they will be safe. Let us find Ameridus and begin the process."

He looked down into the deep green eyes of his eldest daughter, "I will not leave our people to suffer this tragedy alone but I would ask you to organize the best and brightest of our people for this journey. You will be the vanguard of a new culture in a new place."

"But, Father, I can not leave you!"

"My darling, you bear the seed of the *seer*. It is our family that has produced those who can read the ancient texts and it is your destiny to make sure the blessing continues. We know there are other Crystals throughout the world. You must find the right one and then you must start again. The magic that the ancient scribes and *seers* rescued from Atlantis must not be allowed to die or, worse, captured by the barbarians. That is more important than any single civilization. It is a truth that all the world must know someday."

Nanu looked out across the beautiful city. The sacred books and the codex left little doubt that, in a very short time, thousands of years of history would simply disappear. "I will do as you ask but I wish you would come with us."

"I am an old man and I can not, will not leave my people. If they are to perish, then I must stand with them and protect them until the end. That is my duty. I would not be the father that you respect if I chose any other course."

Over the next few days, preparations were made. Four of the finest ships were quietly loaded with provisions for the journey and, on the final night, the sacred book and all of the texts from the temple were moved into the hold of the Princess' ship. At dawn, they sailed with the tide.

Ameridus knocked on Nanu's cabin door, which opened from within by her chambermaid, who was sobbing.

"I am sorry to bother you but we will need to make a decision before we go much farther. Before we left, I entered the Crystal and asked for its guidance. It showed two possible sites for exploration. The first is a large island to the northeast and the second is a smaller island off the northwest coast of our homeland. We can sail to the first island but it would take a major effort to dismantle the ships, move them across the land, reassemble them, and then sail to the second island. I would suggest that we explore the larger island and, if that fails, then we will proceed to the second. I seek your counsel."

Nanu wiped the tears from her eyes, touched by the kindness in Ameridus' exhausted face, "We will sail to the island that lies to the northeast. If that does not serve our purposes, then we will walk to the second island if we have to. Our destiny lies in finding a safe place to rebuild our society and we will not fail." She turned back to her two sisters, who were praying for deliverance.

"As you wish," replied Ameridus, bowing as he backed out of the small cabin.

Ameridus guided the tiny fleet to the exact point where the Crystal was buried. The men were organized to dig a chamber beneath the small mountain and the women built thatched huts high above the shoreline. They found springs for fresh water and the fertile land and a blue-green sea provided an abundance of foods.

As time passed, they improved their tiny village and spring brought many babies. Certainly, it was not as grand as all they left behind but the texts provided guidance and their spirits carried them in the quest to build a new life.

Although Nanu had never been tested in the reading of the ancient texts, Ameridus insisted that she master the writings and, on her first attempt he was not surprised to find that she could interpret the sacred books. She spent several hours of each day studying, under Ameridus' direction, and soon found herself becoming comfortable with these new tasks.

"These books hold the history of our ancestors and the prophesies of our future," said Ameridus. "We would be foolish to find ourselves dependent on only one man to interpret them. It is time for you and your sisters to bear children, so this heritage might be passed on to a new generation."

Nanu protested that she could not marry someone beneath her status but secretly knew that he was right and found herself attracted to the young scribe Protus, who had taken the ancient name when he completed his training. After several months, they married and soon began producing children. Ameridus married Nanu's youngest sister, in spite of the difference in age, and they were blessed with twins.

It was several years before the white devils began to appear. They landed in a large harbor on the south side of the island and were constructing a village to receive ships, navigating to the land of their ancestors and then returning, low in the water, with riches they had plundered.

Ameridus stood before the spinning Crystal, Nanu at his side. They bowed together and turned to leave the sacred chamber. "I fear that it will not be long before the white devils find our little city and destroy what we have built. We must ensure the safety of the texts. It is time to move on."

Nanu looked into his eyes. He had guided their small fleet to this new land and, together, they built the beginnings of a new society. "I fear that I do not have the strength to begin again."

"My dear, I am an old man and you are blessed with the wisdom and the strength of your father. It is I who can not make this journey, which leaves only one possibility. You must lead our people to the island in the Pacific. There is no other choice if our history is to continue."

Nanu accepted the weight of her position but the thought of this next journey alone frightened her. How could she find the strength and wisdom to lead her people on this perilous voyage?

The old man put an arm around her shoulders, "We will consult the texts and I'll provide you with a map that will lead you to the island. I suggest that, when you get there, you name it 'The Island of the Children' as a tribute to our history of hope and to the promise of the next generations."

Nanu buried her face in his robes and wept.

The next morning, the entire population gathered and the plan was discussed at length. The choice was left to each adult or couple, amid unanimous agreement to gather the following morning with their decisions.

Most of the group volunteered to accompany their queen to the new island but several couples decided to stay with Ameridus and Nanu's sister to protect the Crystal. Ameridus insisted that the single copies of the sacred texts would be transported to the new island.

"That leaves you with no guidance," said Nanu, quietly.

"If our civilization is to survive, then The Books must go with you. You are now as well trained and knowledgeable as I and I have absolute faith in your wisdom and your ability to lead our people to safety. Besides, Protus has the gift and your children will surely be blessed. It is as it must be."

Nanu stood at the stern, as the four ships sailed off to the west, and waved to the small group silhouetted on the beach against the rising sun. Ameridus provided a detailed map, from his consultations with the Crystal and the texts that guided them to the narrowest spit of land between the two oceans. Refugees escaping the slaughter of their native people converged to dismantle the ships, transport the timbers across the mountains, and then reconstruct them on the west coast. Several of the original group died during the passage and Nanu filled the ships with as many local people as possible. They sailed up the coast for days and then turned to the west.

The sun was setting as they approached the island that Nanu hoped held the promise of their future. A giant volcanic cone rose up at the north end of the island and the rocks at the top reflected a shimmering red cross against the darkening sky.

Nanu put her arms around Protus' waist and smiled up into his dark eyes. "Perhaps they will never find us here."

"We can only hope."

"This is where we will begin to build our civilization but I must admit that I haven't the strength to move again. Our children are the future and I am hopeful that we will live long enough to see them succeed us."

Protus smiled down at this wife, "You have guided us to safety again and we will build a beautiful city for our people in a place that can not be seen from the sea. Your father would be proud of you."

"I think of him and our homeland often. After talking with the survivors, I fear that he is dead and all that we remember is gone. We must make sure that our people never suffer that conquest again."

"We can only do our best and trust in the texts and this new Crystal to guide us in our quest." Protus hugged Nanu as a blazing orange sun slid below the horizon and the red cross faded into darkness.

Chapter Five

The crew returned to the Jasmine and slowly motored out of the harbor, around the west end of the island, heading south into the Caribbean, through the Panama Canal, and north along the Pacific coast of Mexico.

"The pilot at the canal said that we should have smooth sailing for the next week or so. There are no storms brewing in the Gulf or the Atlantic and the prevailing winds are from the southwest under a high-pressure system. I think we should tally that one to luck. Hopefully, we'll find what we're looking for before the next tempest roars out of the sea," said Travis.

"It's time to retrieve our instrument," said Ponte, with a twinkle in his eye. He disappeared below decks and returned with a wooden box, which he set on the map table in the bridge. "Let's see what she has to say."

He snapped the latches to expose Nanchez' strange sphere, turned several knobs, and crystals began to glow. The meters jumped to life and needles bounced up and down. He turned the instrument to allow the antenna to scan the northern horizon and finally stopped. "The vector is coming from the north-northwest and I'd guess about two hundred miles out."

Travis walked behind Morgan at the wheel and checked the compass.

"North by northwest it is, captain!" cried Morgan, with a broad grin.

Travis laughed and patted her on the back, "I think you're beginning to get this! Let's check the charts as we go. Chances are this island is not included."

"Aye-aye, captain!" said Ian, rolling out the maps on the table.

Ponte was fiddling with his strange round instrument and said, "How about calling home? Shall we try it out?"

The children in the cabin cheered and Kelly ran out onto the deck to call the others in. Ponte pulled a large *messenger* from another box and connected several cables to the instrument. A pulsing blue light glowed from within the *messenger*.

All of the children crowded around as Nanchez' craggy features surrounded the screen, "Ah, Ponte! How are you?"

"We're fine. We're just off the Mexican coast, heading north."

"I know. I've been following your progress through the vectors. I'm surprised you haven't found the tracking device I planted on board before you left!"

"You rascal! No, I haven't found it but I will!"

"How're the children?" inquired Nanchez. "Their parents have been rather concerned about your progress and their safety."

"We're all fine. The children have learned a great deal about celestial navigation, the history of nautical exploration, astronomy, the oceans, and several semesters' worth of history. We're all well. How are things on the Knot?"

"You'd be proud of us. The systems are all functioning normally and I've managed to merge the power supplies between the two Crystals by matching their reverse oscillations. Ester and Alius have been great help."

Nanchez' image suddenly slid to the right, as Ester and Alius shoved him aside, laughing at the giant's hurt expression. "We've been watching your movements!" cried Alius.

"Spies…the lot of you!"

"We've been keeping all of the parents informed. They've been a bit anxious to hear from you," said Ester.

"Ester, M'dear. How are you?"

"I'm fine, dear, and things are progressing nicely on this end. We've set up a little net through the vectors, so the parents can watch, as you've been moving along. You've made good time, although we were all jealous of your time in Jamaica."

"We're almost there, although the island doesn't seem to be on any charts...I wonder why?" chuckled Ponte.

Adrian pushed to the front, "How's my sister *seer*?"

"I'm working at it but it was much easier when there were two of us. At least I haven't had to enter any Crystals since you've been gone," laughed Alius.

"I have complete faith in your gift and wish I was there to help. Hopefully, our mission will be finished in a few days and we can head for home."

"We all miss you!"

"All of us miss you, too. We'll be in touch in as soon as we know our plans."

"Ponte! Our signal is getting weak. Call us when you've landed on the island. The power should be better there..." Nanchez' face distorted and then disappeared. The children groaned and then laughed. It was good to have news that everything on Morgan's Knot was as they left it and, although none of them had time to be homesick, they were relieved to know that their parents would be reassured of their safety.

Ponte set the children to the search for the homing device that Nanchez planted on the ship. After several hours of searching through every nook and cranny, Kelly yelled from the bridge, "I think I've found it!"

Everyone rushed to the bridge to find Kelly holding the ship's compass on her lap. There, in a hallow beneath the breach where the instrument was housed, they found a pulsing red crystal in a small metal housing. Several long white hairs were tied in a tidy bow to a screw on the top of the box.

Ponte removed the box and held it up for inspection, "Very clever, you scallywag!"

"What shall we do with it?" asked Molly.

"M'dear, I think that we'll leave it right where we found it. It has served its purpose well and I see no need to interrupt your parents' sense of security."

———— ⁀⁀⁀ ————

The ship's clock struck midnight with twelve sturdy gongs as Josh and Molly trudged up the ladder to relieve Adrian and Kelly, who were just finishing their last sighting. Molly took the wheel, "What's our heading?"

"Three twenty," replied Kelly, rubbing her eyes.

"Why don't you go to bed," said Adrian. "I'll finish up here."

"Okay," whispered the little blond, as she hugged each of her friends in turn and traipsed down the ladder.

Josh leaned over the chart, watching Adrian plot their position. "Looks like we'll be there by morning."

"Just about daybreak," replied Adrian. "Weather's clear and the seas are calm."

"We can take it from here," said Molly.

Adrian turned from the wheelhouse and noticed the Professor standing at the stern, his feet planted wide, hands clasped behind his back. He was staring up at Jupiter. Sensing the young *seer* behind him, he said, "The sky is so clear that you could almost see the moons of Jupiter with your bare eyes. It would be lovely to have a decent telescope along."

"It might be tough to keep it trained on anything," laughed Adrian.

"With proper gyroscopes, perhaps..." mused Ponte.

The young *seer* gazed at the giant planet glowing in the darkness, "Tell me about *seers*."

The Professor turned and stared at his pupil, "What is it that you want to know?"

"From your stories and what I've learned in my brief introduction to the Books, I hope there are other *seers* and Keepers working with Crystals all over the planet but, sometimes, I feel that Alius and I are the only ones who have these talents. We both sense there is so much more…"

"I've studied the Powers since I was a child and I'm confident that there are others, just like us, working on the same problems and probably finding better solutions, especially after our encounter with the old man in the market. I also believe that there are as many working with the Dark Crystals."

He was quiet for a moment, "The Powers were harnessed at the dawn of man for good and evil, just as there are those who follow a righteous path and others who succumb to their weaknesses. Those who guard the secrets hold the future of the world in their hands. There's plenty of evil in the world and maybe it's up to us to defend the blessings that we all share on this planet."

"Tic said that there is a responsibility that goes with this new talent of mine…at a price more dear than I might ever imagine. I don't mind the responsibility part but I wish that I had some hint about the rest of it. There's more to this than just using the powers to maintain our standard of living."

"I believe there is much more and, perhaps, we'll be fortunate enough to learn some of it together. Our history is filled with fables and myths about armies from the Light and the Dark engaging in gargantuan battles that raged on for centuries until there was a temporary victor or stalemate. Then the warriors would fade back to the safety and comfort of their Crystals to rebuild life until the next conflict. I'm not sure how the troops were roused from places like Morgan's Knot. I've certainly never received a signal from our brethren."

"You'd think that everyone would want to know about everyone else."

"That's true for you and me but I'm sure that, if they exist, there is a good reason for their anonymity."

"That's not a satisfying answer!"

"No, it's not but, if you believe in the Powers, then you believe that this magic touches everyone everywhere. According to the legend of Atlantis, those scribes delivered their texts to the far corners of the Earth. Besides, we both know that the more we learn, the more we find there is to learn. It is never-ending and, perhaps, that's a good thing."

"I doubt that it will ever be boring."

"Laddie, you've got that right," laughed the Professor.

"But you still haven't answered my question."

Ponte paused, knuckle to his lips, "That's true. I have to admit that our little world has been a closed environment since long before I was born and the primary concentration of our efforts has been to maintain and improve our use of the Powers on the island. I've always wondered, hoped, that there were others like us and, someday, we might discover each other. From what I've learned over the past few weeks, I'm positive there are others out there and, somehow, we'll find them."

"As to someone, you for instance, being a *seer*, I think my opinion has changed on that too. I'm afraid that I've been terribly selfish in my use of the *seers* at my disposal, asking each of you to interpret for me rather than developing and expanding your own potential. So my...definition...has matured..." he paused again. "I think that a master *seer* would have to be guided by the wisdom of the ancients to lead our people, our world into the Balance. There is also a fear, someplace deep within my soul, crying out that it is equally probable that there are forces dedicated to the Dark Crystals and, if human nature is any indication, they will stop at nothing to exercise their power. I fear those legends of grand battles between good and evil will prove far more real than either of us might hope."

"That's not exactly what I wanted to hear..."

"That's not exactly what I intended to tell you, knowing this conversation would come up sooner or later, but I fear that I've been far too isolated, certainly blind to the rest of the world. No, I do apologize for my honesty but there is my hope that, over time, you will master these innate talents of yours and expand your knowledge so that you might become a leader with a conscience."

"This is more than reading from ancient books and playing with cool technology, isn't it?"

The Professor laughed, "Aye, my boy, I'm afraid that you've been saddled with a relentless responsibility that will follow you around like an old dog until your time is done. Even if we find your parents and you move on to Vancouver, you'll always belong in this world...but then, you already knew that didn't you?"

John and Sara awoke from their drug-induced stupor lashed to two stakes before an open chasm that fell away into darkness. Fires burned in open pits and voices chanted in murmurs while drums thumped a hypnotic beat around them. The sturdy wooden posts were planted in the middle of a plaza in the midst of the ruins of a small city at the base of a mountain. Vines and trees grew through what remained of ghostly white stone buildings, abandoned centuries before.

Behind the pit, a single white column rose above the smooth stone surface of the square, topped with a large red crystal pulsing rhythmically with the drums. Beyond the pillar, an ancient step pyramid rose out of the jungle into the night, its shape imitating a conical peak behind it.

A boy suddenly appeared directly in front of the column. He was dressed in a loincloth, his skin and hair dull gray, "As dictated by the Book of Natural Balance, no person of maturity may inhabit this island. You will be delivered to the underworld. This is as it has always been."

The murmurs erupted into cheers as the boy walked between them and disappeared. The red Crystal suddenly glowed with a fierce red radiance and the two posts tipped forward and began to descend into the abyss. Sara screamed, "I love you."

"I love you, too," yelled John, as they dropped into darkness.

George, Ponte, and Josh leaned over Nanchez' strange but brilliant instrument. "It should be just to the northwest," said Josh, as Travis took the wheel from Molly and slowed the Jasmine to a crawl.

"Land-ho!" yelled Kelly, from her perch on top of the cabin, as Magnus flew off to survey the island.

Everyone scrambled up on deck for a better view. It seemed larger than Morgan's Knot and there was a huge, conical mountain rising from the north, with a series of serrated ridges cascading to the south.

"That mountain was created by a volcano," instructed the Professor.

Travis yelled from the bridge, "How do you want to approach?"

"Let's circumnavigate it and see if there is any sign of life or a good place to put in," replied Ponte.

Travis followed the coastline around the north side of the island, which was lush with growth and offered only steep volcanic cliffs, then down the west side. The Professor brought out a pair of binoculars but there was no evidence of movement or habitation on the island. They found a small bay with a narrow entry on the west side but Travis was hesitant to put in until they had explored the depth of the water. They continued around a jagged dagger diving beneath the waves on the south end of the island and Travis slowed to a dead crawl as they came back around to the east side. "There's that small cove on the west side of the island but I'm not sure how deep it is and I think that we might be wise to drop anchor out here and take the skiff to the beach. Josh and Ian, prepare to drop anchor!"

"Right you are, then," replied Ponte. "Children, let's lower the lifeboat and we'll send a party to scout this part of the island."

George and the children set to work. Josh and Ian dropped the anchor, as Travis turned the Jasmine into the wind. The rest of the children rigged the little boat, lowered it over the port side, and tied off a line to a cleat on the stern.

"We can't take everyone," said Ponte. "I'll take Adrian, Megan, Morgan, and Josh in first and, after we've had a chance to look around, we'll send the boat back for the rest of you. Is that alright with you, Travis?"

"Certainly, someone should stay with the boat anyway. The rest of you can help get things stowed away while we wait and, while we're anchored, I could use George's expertise with that starboard engine."

Ian and Morgan climbed over the side and slid down into the dinghy. Adrian and Megan helped Ponte lift his rather generous girth over the side and then followed him to their places at the oars. Kelly untied the line and threw it to Megan, as the lifeboat moved away from the Jasmine, "Good hunting!"

They beached the boat and tethered the line to a rock that jutted from the sand on the shore. There was no sign of movement along the dunes, so they made their way up to the forest of palm trees and scrub that lined the shore and found no easy entry. "Let's follow the beach and see if we can find tracks or a trail," said Adrian.

They moved off to the north and, after walking for a few minutes, found two sets of adult boot prints in the sand leading from the water to the beach and then back again. They were not fresh but at the point where the tracks retreated to the sea, they found several smaller footprints leading into the bush and two sets of adult prints, one larger and heavier, the other smaller and lighter, that led up a small hill just to the north.

There were no open trails entering the thick jungle, so they followed the adult footprints until they found an encampment and a tree house in a giant banyan tree. There were two woven palm plates lying on the sand and more footprints leading off into the trees. Josh and Megan scrambled up the tree to explore the structure. Megan leaned over the edge and yelled down, "I think that we've found something!"

They slid down the rope ladder and held up a small locket. "I think this might be a good sign," said his cousin, handing the golden chain to Adrian.

He took it hesitantly and held it up to inspect it. He had never seen it before.

"Open it," yelled Josh from the tree house.

Adrian opened the small clasp and stared at a tiny photograph of himself. He smiled broadly and whispered, "They're here somewhere!"

Ponte patted him on the back and smiled, "I think we can send for the rest of the crew. We'll make our camp here and see if they return. Josh, you and Megan take the dinghy back to the Jasmine and bring George and the rest of the children as well as Brandy and Tic. Travis will want to stay with the boat but tell him what we've found. Oh, I've left a small leather bag and two wooden boxes of instruments next to my bunk, would you bring them to me?"

"Okay," said Josh, as he and Megan ran down the beach to the little boat. Within thirty minutes, the skiff returned and the children tied off the line to the rock on the beach. Brandy jumped into the water before they made it to the beach and swam the rest of the way. He shook himself off and ran up and down the beach panting, "Dry land! It feels so good to run!"

Molly carried Tic through the surf and set him on the sand. He kicked up one foot after the other, "Sand! I hate sand, unless it's in a cat box!"

Josh carried the Professor's leather bag and Kelly held Ian's hand, as they walked up the beach to meet Ponte and the other children. She was looking a little bit hesitant.

Morgan bent down to Kelly, "What's wrong?"

"I don't know. I have a funny feeling about this place!"

"Don't be afraid. We'll find Adrian's parents and then we'll head for home, promise!"

Kelly spied the tree house and scrambled up the tree, "This is great! Just like in the storybooks!"

"Where's George?" inquired Adrian.

"He's helping Travis with that starboard engine and asked that we send the skiff back out in a little while," replied Molly.

Ponte took the bag from Josh and boxes from Ian to begin assembling several pieces of equipment on the sand. As he connected one to the next, crystals began to glow and one unit began to hum. The Professor thumped it with his hand and it quieted. He studied the gauges and adjusted the dials for several minutes. "Well, the vectors are strong here. It seems that the primary Crystal is somewhere in or near the mountain. The energy from the second Crystal is much weaker. I would guess that it's somewhere off the coast and the water is interfering with the signal."

Adrian peered over the Professor's shoulder but he didn't understand what the instruments were showing, "I wonder whether there was a Book of Wisdoms here?"

"Well, we've seen footprints that might be those of your parents and the other prints seem to be made by children or very small people. We'll have to do a bit of exploring."

Brandy was sniffing around the campsite, "I smell your parents but there are lots of other human scents around here too."

Ponte gathered the children together. "Adrian, you take Morgan, Molly, and Tic and begin to explore to the north. Josh, you, Ian, Megan, and Brandy can go to the south. Don't go too far, for the moment. We're looking for any sign of a path that leads into the forest. If you find anything come straight back. Kelly and I will wait here, in case your parents return."

The children broke into groups and began to move along the edge of the thick forest. Tic bounded ahead of Adrian and the girls and disappeared. The undergrowth was dense and their movements were slow until they were about one hundred yards from the beach, where the thick growth opened to a small clearing beneath tall palms and pines.

Banyan trees and other smaller varieties grew in those patches where the sun peaked through the canopy to touch the ground. Giant ferns erupted from the soil amid thickets of tiny bamboo twisting the perception of large and small.

Tic sat on a rock, licking his paws, "There are animal tracks leading in several directions. It seems that something was dragged over this path to the north. The trail smells of humans."

Adrian and the girls squatted down on the path. Tic was right, the dirt and pine needles were brushed away from the middle of the path and there were two continuous grooves leading away through the trees.

Tic stared up into the trees and meowed loudly. The children followed the old tomcat's gaze to a beautiful parrot squawking back in response. The conversation went back and forth for several minutes before Tic finally said, "The animals on this island don't speak with the humans but the parrot told me that the children took the adults to the city."

"The children? What city?" inquired Adrian.

"That's what he said."

"Ask him about the city."

Tic meowed and the parrot squawked for a few minutes. Finally, Tic turned to Adrian and said, "The parrot says that there are remains of an ancient city near the base of the mountain and there are children living on this island!"

"Children? What about adults?"

"The parrot says that no adults live on the island."

"Let's go back and tell the Professor what we've found."

The children pushed through the undergrowth towards the tree house and were surprised to find no sign of Ponte and Kelly. The Professor's instruments were still sitting on the sand, the crystals still glowing. Morgan climbed up to the tree house but found no one. Adrian put his fingers in his mouth and whistled as loud as he could. There was no response.

"I wonder where they've gone, it's not like the Professor to wander off and Kelly was too scared to go exploring."

"They'll be back. Whistle again. Let's see if we can find Josh, Ian, and Megan," replied Morgan. "Surely Brandy will hear you."

Adrian whistled several times but, again, there was no response. He walked over to the Professor's equipment and noticed something shiny in the sand, reaching down to pick up a bracelet of beautiful little shells. His friends gathered around, "I bought this for Kelly at the market in Jamaica. The clasp is broken."

Magnus flew in, "I found the ruins on an ancient city on the other side of the island but it's hidden from the sea. There's a smoking firepit in the middle of the square but I didn't actually see any humans."

"Thanks," said Morgan. "As soon as we talk with George, we'll head out."

The skiff was still tied to a rock on the beach. They turned to the Jasmine and waved to Travis and George, who were standing on the deck behind the bridge. George waved for them to bring the dinghy back to pick him up.

Farther out over the water, a huge black cloud billowed up out of the sea, trailing a drenching rain and brilliant crackles of lightning. They waved and pointed to the approaching storm. Travis saluted and turned into the boat to close up the hatches as the squall closed on the trawler. Within a few minutes, the mysterious cloud was hovering right above the craft, although there was sunshine and calm on the beach.

A huge clap of thunder rolled along the shore and lightning formed a ring of electrical fire from the clouds to the surface of the water, engulfing the Jasmine.

As suddenly as it appeared, the storm faded and the clouds disappeared. The boat had vanished. The waves on the ocean returned to a light chop and the wind was calm. Adrian turned to his companions, with a look of astonishment.

"The boat...it's gone!" gasped Molly.

Magnus flew out to circle the area and returned, "There's nothing out there, no debris and no shadow beneath the water."

"I don't believe what we just witnessed!" exclaimed Morgan.

"There has to be a reasonable explanation for what just happened. Let's see if we can find Josh and the rest of the crew," replied Adrian. "Tic, see if you can find Brandy's scent."

Tic ran to the spot where the other children entered the jungle and ran beneath the underbrush into the trees. Adrian and the girls followed, pushing through the sea grape, razor grass, and scrub palms growing in the dunes. Again, the brush opened beneath a canopy of huge trees and, other than the calls and songs of birds, the jungle was silent.

Tic was waiting, "The track leads off to the north and I smell other human scents. The other children are not alone…and I sense that we are being watched."

The children looked around but they couldn't see anything or anyone through the dense jungle.

"We have no choice. We have to follow them. Tic lead the way," said Adrian.

They moved off along a narrow animal track through the trees. Tic stopped, occasionally, to point out broken twigs and branches. "These indicate that whoever came through here was moving in this direction."

He picked up the scent and trotted along the path. It was hot and humid, which slowed their progress. After an hour, they came to a small stream and waded into the cool water. Adrian scooped up a handful of the cool liquid and tasted it, "It's fresh water!"

Molly sat on a flat rock at the edge of the stream dangling her feet, "This reminds me of our place in the forest at home. I wish all of our animal friends were here!"

"We sure could use their help," added Morgan.

Tic turned, suddenly, and stared into the darkness of the jungle. "Not all of the animals in the world are friendly. I think we should get out of here, NOW!"

A small herd of wild boar scampered out of the trees, eyeing the children sitting in the watering hole, snorting loudly and scuffing the dirt like angry bulls warning of an impending charge. The children leapt to their feet, Molly grabbed Tic, and charged downstream.

They walked for a half hour before they stumbled into a thicket of bushes covered with berries. Adrian found two coconuts and broke one open on a rock. He passed pieces to Molly and Morgan and shared the berries they collected. He poked the eyes of the second coconut with his penknife and poured some of the milk into a piece of shell for Tic. "I'm sorry it's not real milk but it's the best that we can do for the moment."

Tic lapped the milk from the shell, "You're right, it would be better if it was real milk but this isn't bad. Thank you."

Golden sunlight skimmed across the canopy of the forest but the floor was growing dark.

"We must be getting close to the mountain," said Molly.

"I sure hope so, my feet are tired!" replied Morgan.

"I've been thinking about our next move," said Adrian. "I think that we should get off this path and find our way through the trees. Whoever took the Professor and the other children must know we're here."

"I agree," said Morgan. "I just wish we knew what we're about to face. Are there *others* on the island or do they think that we are some kind of aliens?"

"We're strangers in a strange land. I wish we had access to the Book of Wisdoms for some guidance. Tic, have you had any sense that we're being watched?"

"Other than the monkey that's sitting in that tree above your head, no."

Adrian leaned back and looked up into the tree. There was a monkey staring down at him. "Hey, fella, do you speak English?"

The monkey made squeaky noises and climbed down closer to the children. Tic meowed and the monkey responded. The conversation lasted for several minutes before Tic turned to the children and said, "He wants to know why you are wearing these strange clothes and whether you're a part of the tribe. I told him that we're new to this island and he said that the tribe had passed through here about an hour ago with other children, a dog, and an older man dressed like you."

"Ask him where they've gone."

Tic meowed and the monkey squeaked back and forth. "He says that they've gone to the city and that Ponte, Brandy, and the children were bound."

Adrian exchanged anxious looks with the two girls. "How far is the village?"

"It's not far to the north," replied Tic.

"I'll go scout it again," squawked Magnus, extending his wings to leap silently into the air.

"We'd best get moving," said Molly. "Maybe we can make them understand that we mean them no harm and are only here to find your parents."

"I have a feeling that they don't care why we're here. From their point of view, we're invaders," whispered Morgan.

"We have no choice," said Adrian. "Let's go."

The monkey scrambled down the tree to within a few feet of the children. He squeaked several times and Tic translated, "He says that he knows the way and he'll guide us."

"Great!" exclaimed Molly, "We can use all the help we can get!"

The monkey took the lead and moved into the forest. They began to catch glimpses of the silhouette of the mountain rising up above the trees and noticed that the rocks at the top of the peak were glowing a deep red in reflection of the waning sun. Adrian stopped the procession and turned to Tic, "Ask the monkey whether there's a place where they could see the city without being seen."

The two animals conversed for a few minutes before Tic said, "Yes, but we'll have to stay in the shadows of the forest. The monkey says that the 'ghost children' have spotters along the paths."

"What are ghost children?" asked Morgan.

After a few squeaks and meows, Tic replied, "They are the children that inhabit this island."

"Are there no grown-ups?" asked Molly.

"Evidently not, it seems that adults are not allowed to live on the island."

"Does our monkey have a name?" inquired Adrian.

"Yes, his name is Blackbeard!"

"Blackbeard? Where did he get a name like that?"

The monkey squeaked.

"He says that it's a long story and we should get moving," replied Tic. "He's right. If we're going to get to the city below the mountain before it gets completely dark, we better get started."

Blackbeard climbed down from his perch in the tree and scrambled off through the trees to their left. Tic and the monkey climbed under or over the obstructions in their path and the children clamored to keep up. Presently, the animals crested a small hill and settled beneath low branches of the trees at the top of the ridge.

The children peered down the slope overlooking the remains of what must have been a beautiful little city. They could make out the ruins of many stone buildings and the stumps of classically formed columns surrounding what might have been a public plaza. Beyond the square, a pyramid rose out of the jungle. The sides of the structure were stepped like the pyramids in Central America in Adrian's geography book.

Fires burned in pits around the edges of the square and a semi-circle of children faced the pyramid. Brandy and their friends were connected to one another with collars and rope, while Ponte was tied to a wooden stake facing a white column before a dark circle in the ground. A tall boy, with gray skin and a loincloth, walked in front of Ponte and seemed to address the group. There were, perhaps, sixty or seventy ghost children on the plaza. He walked back to the semi-circle just as the post holding Ponte began to tip forward into an open pit.

Adrian screamed, "Nooooo!" and scrambled down the hill as Magnus dove out of the darkness with a mighty screech and talons extended.

Blackbeard reached a hand to stop Tic, as the two girls followed, "Stay here. You don't want to be caught by the ghost children. We are delicacies to them."

The two animals watched as the semi-circle turned and closed on Adrian and the girls.

Chapter Six

The ghost children overwhelmed the intruders, tied their hands behind their backs, and secured rope collars around their necks. They marched from the plaza through the forest to a colossal cave in the base of the mountain, flanked on either side by children, some older, some younger, but all covered in gray.

Megan, Ian, Josh, and Kelly slumped against the stonewall on the opposite side of the fire from Adrian. They stared blankly and did not react when he whistled or rolled into their line of sight. Brandy was tied to a ring in the cave wall next to the other children. He was sound asleep and did not stir when the latest group of prisoners arrived.

The ghost children ranged from three or four years old to eleven or twelve. None had reached maturity. They tied a rope through the collars of their captives and attached it to the ring in the stone. Other children were busy cooking over a fire near the mouth of the cavern and presently brought woven palm platters of food to their captives.

The ropes that bound their hands were untied and plates placed before them. Adrian leaned over to Morgan and whispered, "Don't eat! I think they've drugged our friends."

Morgan relayed the message to Molly, who pulled back from the food at her fingertips. Their friends ate mechanically, their eyes glazed and unfocused, but, being famished, it took every ounce of restraint to keep from reaching out for just one bite.

Presently, a tall boy stood over Adrian, "Why don't you eat?" He wore a loincloth and sun-bleached curls cascaded down his back but his skin was gray.

"I'm not hungry," replied Adrian. "What have you done to our friends?"

"They're alright. They'll recover. Eat!"

Adrian kicked over his plate with his foot and stared up at the boy defiantly.

The boy smiled, "You'll learn." He turned and walked away.

After dinner, they watched their friends topple over into a sound sleep. Adrian leaned over to the girls, "See, they've put something in the food."

Morgan and Molly both nodded.

"Sooner or later, we'll have to eat and drink. I'm not sure how long I can hold out."

"I know but, between now and then, we have to learn what's happening here and convince the ghost children that we're not a threat to them," said Adrian quietly.

Presently, two young girls brought wooden cups filled with water and placed them before their captives. Morgan said quietly, "Are there only children on this island?"

One of the young girls nodded and looked at her companion for guidance, "Adults are forbidden to live on the island."

"Why?"

"It is written," said the other girl.

"Where is it written?" inquired Adrian.

"It is as it has always been," said the other girl, walking away to rejoin the group sitting around the fire near the entrance to the cave.

The ghost children talked quietly and Adrian and the girls noticed that they were speaking a combination of several languages. Molly suggested that it was partly English and partly Spanish. Morgan thought that she heard a bit of French and another language that might have been Asian.

After a while, the tall boy returned and stood before them, "You must eat and drink."

"We don't want to end up like our friends over there," said Molly.

"They'll recover," said the tall boy.

"We came here to rescue my parents. We mean no harm to you," said Adrian, studying the boy's eyes.

"The blond woman and the big man? They've been passed to the underworld."

"Is that where you sent our friend, the older man?"

"Yes. No mature person may stay on the island. It is written and it is as it has always been."

"Where is it written," inquired Morgan.

"In the Book of Natural Balance."

The boy began to walk away when Adrian asked, "What happened to your parents?"

The boy turned back to Adrian, "Most of us were left here by pirates. We don't know what happened to our parents."

"I'm sorry, that must be hard," said Morgan.

"We've learned how to survive. We learn from each other. The older children care for the younger ones. It is as it has always been."

"How long has this been going on," asked Molly?

"I don't know, for as long as pirates have been leaving children on this island."

"What happens when you reach maturity?" asked Adrian.

"I'll be cast to the underworld, like those before me."

"Why?" inquired Molly.

"As I said, it is written and it is as it has always been," The boy turned back to his companions.

After a while, the entire tribe curled up on the floor of the cave and went to sleep. Adrian and the girls struggled to remove the collars from around their necks but the knots would not budge. He reached into his pocket to withdraw his little pocketknife and, after a long quiet struggle, freed himself and set to work on the girls. Before he could finish, the ghost children were standing over them. Their collars were replaced and their hands bound behind their backs. The tall boy took the knife, flashed the blade in front of Adrian's face, and walked away.

The next morning, Adrian rolled into a sitting position to find Molly and Morgan still asleep but their friends were sitting in a row on the opposite side of the cave. Megan stared at Adrian with an expression of disbelief, her eyes struggling to focus.

He mouthed, "Don't eat."

Megan smiled as if she were just seeing him.

Again, he mouthed but didn't speak aloud, "Don't eat."

Megan frowned as if she were considering his words. After a while, she nodded and leaned over to Ian, who whispered to Kelly, who looked up with a quizzical frown and whispered to Josh.

The ghost children were busy cooking over the fire near the mouth of the cave and presently brought plates to their captives. Their hands were untied but the prisoners did not attempt to eat the food on the woven plates or to drink the juice in the wooden cups.

The tall boy walked over and stood before Adrian. "You can eat this food. It will not harm you."

"You drugged our friends. How do we know that you haven't put something in this food?"

"You have only my word."

"And why should we believe you?"

The boy produced the knife and touched the blade to Adrian's cheek, "I could cut you but I'm going to remove your collar. Don't resist."

He cut the tether from Adrian's neck and then proceeded to free the rest of the prisoners. He reached down, picked up the plate in front of Adrian, took a bit of pineapple for himself, and handed it back, "Eat."

Adrian picked up the plate, looked to his friends for approval, and took a bite of the fish. The rest of the children picked up the food and ate ravenously. When they finished, two young girls retrieved their plates and the tall boy walked over and sat down in front of Adrian.

"There is no escape from this island. We know how to survive in this jungle. If you join us, we will teach you. If you go off on your own, you'll probably die."

"Fair enough," replied Adrian.

"Let me tell you the story of the Island of the Children."

Adrian's friends huddled around the tall boy to hear the tale.

"Generations ago, pirates captured and plundered trading ships that passed through these waters. The men who survived were given the choice of joining the pirates or walking the plank. The women were sold as slaves. The pirates had no use for the children and they were of little value as slaves, but, in a strange way, they were bound by a peculiar code that banned harming a child. They also had no use for animals they could not eat, so the easy answer to their predicament was to leave the animals and the children to fend for themselves on an island. This island."

"Each time their ships passed La Isla de los Ninos, they would cast off the younger children and retrieve those who had matured. The older boys were put to work on the ships or sold as slaves but the pirates were primarily interested in the girls."

"Each new group of children was taken in by those who lived on the island and taught the lessons that would allow them to survive. The older children taught the younger children and the lessons were passed down through the years. The only way to keep the pirates from kidnapping the older children was to sacrifice them to the keepers of the underworld. That way, the only inhabitants of this island were young children."

Adrian interrupted, "Is that what you did with our friend last night?"

"Yes. He is with the keepers of the underworld."

"Who are these keepers?"

"We don't know. We've never seen them. It is as it has always been."

"Are you saying that there are pirates who continue this tradition to this day?"

"Yes," he said, turning to point. "See that boy and girl sitting in the corner over there? They were left on the beach a few weeks ago. They'll come around but, at the moment, they are very sad. Most of us were left by pirates, although some children just appear in the city. They are always very young."

Adrian looked around at his friends, each mesmerized by the story, and stared at the boy for several moments, "What's your name?"

"I am Raffe. I was one of the children that just appeared. I don't have any memory of my parents or where I came from."

"I'm sorry about that," replied Adrian. "I have another question. Why do you cover yourselves with ashes?"

"It has been our custom to appear as ghosts. The pirates seem to be afraid of the supernatural and perhaps they think that we are children who died as a result of being left on this island. We have scouts on the ridge to warn us when they are within sight and we prepare."

The boy stood up, "As I said, you can join us and we'll teach you or you can go off on your own but know that the forest is full of wild animals that would eat you at the first opportunity. Evidently, one group of pirates attacked a ship carrying circus animals and didn't know what to do with them, so they left them here."

Kelly piped up, pointing towards the entrance to the cave, "You mean like those animals?"

Amid screams of panic, the ghost children stampeded to the back of the cavern. Adrian turned to ghostly silhouettes in the glare at the mouth of the cave. Raffe pressed against the wall, edging carefully to the entrance behind the group from Morgan's Knot. The clearing was filled with enough animals to stock several circuses, all sitting or standing very still, and at front of the group sat Tic, licking his paws with complete nonchalance.

There were all sorts of animals…monkeys, chimpanzees, wild boar, mountain goats, bears, lions, tigers, panthers, jaguars, cheetahs, elephants, two giraffes with a gangly youngster, zebras, several horses and ponies, a few cows, sheep, dogs, cats, squirrels, snakes, iguanas, two armadillo, mice, rats, a packet of porcupines, raccoons, gazelle, and birds of every color and size. Brandy ran outside and licked the top of Tic's head with a big slurp. The quiet was broken by a might caw from Magnus.

Raffe was frozen somewhere between awe and terror. Adrian reached out and touched his arm, "It's okay, we have a different relationship with the animals. Let me go have a chat with them."

"Talk with them?"

"Sure, watch." Adrian walked out through the mouth of the cave into the sunshine and picked the old cat up in his arms, "I should have known that you'd come to our rescue!"

"I've had practice," replied Tic.

Morgan and the other children followed Adrian outside. The ghost children were hesitant to leave the safety of the cave but, one by one, crept out into the sunshine.

Tic translated for Adrian, "My friends, we come from a place where the animals and the humans work together in perfect harmony. We're here to encourage the balance between man and nature...in this case, between the animal kingdom and these children. I ask you to guard these young people from harm by anyone attempting to land on this island. In return, there will be no more hunting."

The animals nodded their heads in understanding and mooed, whinnied, barked, and growled their approval. The ghost children moved closer under a brilliant cloud of birds following Magnus and circling the clearing.

"We've witnessed the harmony that can and should exist throughout our world, the lessons that each side can learn from the other, and the paradise that can grow from this union. This is the promise of our home and we hope that you'll join us in making it a reality here."

There was a deafening roar as the animals gathered around the children. Blackbeard scampered over to climb Raffe's leg and wrapped his arms around his neck. Adrian turned and said, "This is The Balance. You'll find that these creatures will become your friends, your protectors, and your allies, if you treat them with the respect they deserve."

"We've always been afraid of the animals in the forest but we'd rather have them as friends. I understand that we have much to learn from you about this balance. We'll agree to stop hunting."

The animals roared. Adrian, his friends, and Raffe walked into the throng of animals and petted each animal in turn. The rest of the ghost children followed and soon giggles and laughter echoed across the plaza, as the neighbors introduced themselves for the first time.

Raffe collected Todd, Sandy, and the children from Morgan's Knot for a tour of the island. Brandy, Tic, and Blackbeard wandered in and out of the jungle along the path and Magnus soared just above the treetops.

"If we follow the ridge line, there are perches where we can see both sides of the island. The area to the north of the mountain falls off into the ocean but there's a waterfall not too far from here. Let's start there."

From a clearing on top of the ridge, they could see the sandy beach, to the east, where they put ashore. The ocean was blue-green, an endless sheet of shimmering sparkles in the afternoon sun. Long slow swells rolled through the spot where the Jasmine had been anchored but no one commented because each was wondering about the fate of George and Travis and their ride home.

The children followed Raffe through the jungle to a deep blue lagoon beneath a shimmering waterfall. Flowers in a rainbow of colors burst from the lush green growth flowing down the banks to touch the pond. They all jumped into the clear water and swung on vines hanging from trees, arching over the tiny lake.

Blackbeard kept shaking his finger, as if scolding the children on their form. He shook his head from side to side and grabbed a vine. With a perfect swing, he let go at the top of the arc into a double back flip and landed next to Morgan with a mighty splash. He bobbed to the surface, smiling from ear to ear.

The children cheered.

"I think all of you have just been shown the proper form," said Tic, who was sitting on a rock in the shade watching the demonstration.

Brandy swam from one child to the next like a maroon motorboat, "I didn't mind life on the trawler but this is a much better use of water!"

After a while, they all trouped out of the pool and moved off to the west. They climbed several ridges and descended through narrow valleys before arriving on the cliffs overlooking the cove.

Raffe laughed, "Listen to this!" He yelled, "Hello!" and the rocks surrounding the bay reflected an echo of his voice that seemed much louder than his original call. They took turns yelling into the inlet and listening to the reverberations.

"It sure makes your voice sound much louder, much bigger than in real life," commented Todd. "We sound like giants!"

"We saw this cove when we first arrived at the island. How deep is it?" asked Adrian.

"It's deep enough for pleasure craft, probably fifteen or twenty feet. The rocky ledge is a great place for crabbing," replied Raffe. "Occasionally, people will pull in for the night and climb the cliffs. I often wonder whether ancient ships put in here."

"I wouldn't doubt it," said Molly. "It's protected from the sea and the rocks that jut up around the entrance would prevent anyone from seeing anchored boats."

"I still wonder where they found the rock to build the city. It's different than the stone that we're seeing along this ridge or in the mountain," pondered Ian. "How'd they transport it across the island? It would have been impossible to haul those stones up these cliffs."

"Maybe they just pulled up to the beach and unloaded it," smiled Kelly.

Everyone laughed at the obvious solution.

"Let's get moving. I want to show you the view from the south end of the ridge," said Raffe. "I'm not sure that Todd and Sandy have seen this."

Sandy whispered, "No, I haven't been to the south end of the island yet."

She had been sullen since they left the plaza and Morgan walked next to her, as they set off over several hills and into ravines along a path climbing to the crest of the ridge. "It must be hard, losing track of your parents."

"It is. I'm pretty sure we won't see them again. Those pirates were scary people. We were kinda surprised they didn't kill us."

"That must have been a terrifying experience. I know it's not a good substitute but the children on this island seem to behave as if they're one big family," whispered Morgan.

Tears streamed down Sandy's cheeks, "They've been very kind and they've respected our need to mourn, to be sad. Some of them have been through the same experience and none of their parents ever came back to find them. They're all still here."

Morgan put an arm around her shoulders. There was nothing that she could say to make her new friend feel better but the innocence and calm of Morgan's Knot seemed implausible in the brutality of the real world.

They walked through the dense jungle and climbed rocky slopes for an hour. The animals of the jungle followed their movements and the woods echoed with the songs of birds, the growls of big cats, and all the sounds of the rain forest.

Blackbeard decided that riding on Raffe's back was far preferable to walking or climbing through the trees and he reached out to touch whoever was walking close by. He seemed fascinated with the curls in Molly and Megan's hair and grabbed a handful whenever they got too near.

"Stop that, you mangy monkey. That hurts!" squealed Molly.

"He thinks you're pretty," joked Josh.

"I think that he's pretty cute too, as long as he's not pulling my hair!"

Blackbeard laughed and pursed his lips together, making kissing sounds at Molly.

They scrambled up a large boulder and stood together at the top. From here, they could see both coasts, the south tip of the island, and the blue-green ocean stretching on to the horizon in every direction. Magnus' silhouette crossed the blazing sun, low in the west, and hot colors rippled across the water, a barrage of flashes firing off in some beautiful, random pattern on the waves.

Megan pointed to several patches of flat, level land along the east side of the ridge. "Those areas look like the fields around the House of the Four Seasons. I wonder whether the ancient people farmed this part of the island?"

"Well, they had to produce food, so you're probably on to something. We should explore that before we head for home," replied Morgan.

To the north, the tip of the mountain erupted above the ridge, shining with a fierce red glow. Adrian could feel the power, "This is a magical island. There are Crystals here and we'll find the underworld and the solution to the riddle of the pirates. I can feel it."

They started back along the path, then down through one of the fields that Megan spotted. The land was fairly level in the meadow, which covered several acres bounded by lines of boulders sticking up through the ground. Water trickled down from a crag in the rocks and filled a shallow stone trough along the west side of the flat pasture. Vines and bushes covered the center and yellow and purple flowers bloomed around the edges. Morgan reached down and took a handful of soil, squeezing it gently, "This is perfect for growing crops."

Megan found a cluster of plants that resembled the young cotton growing in the south fields at home and, along the edge of the next field, they found corn growing wild, "These fields were planted by people. They grew food, just like we do at home."

A grove of sugarcane arched over the little stream and Raffe broke off a stock, grabbed a rock to crush the cane, and handed out pieces to each of the children.

"This is more fun than candy," cried Molly.

"Wouldn't Mum love this," smirked Megan.

Ian and Josh were walking along the edge of the pool, when something shiny caught Ian's eye. He waded into the water and reached down to pick up the object. It appeared to be piece of a flat medallion, and, on the surface, he could barely make out the inlaid image of a crescent moon surrounding two arms of a perfect cross.

"Hey, Adrian!" yelled Josh, "I think Ian's found something interesting."

All of the children gathered around to inspect the charm. "That looks like the pendant that the old man in the market was wearing around his neck when I bought my material," said Morgan.

"He said that it was the ancient symbol for the *seer*," replied Adrian.

"What is a *seer*?" asked Todd.

"A *seer* is a person who can read from the ancient texts," replied Kelly. "Adrian is a *seer*."

"So, this talent of yours, being a *seer*, is it possessed by other people in the world?" asked Raffe.

"Yes, I've been told that the gift is inherited through the mother's bloodline. A *seer* can be male or female but only a woman can pass along the trait. I had no idea I was a *seer* until I took the test on Morgan's Knot. I'm glad to have this ability but it was very strange, learning I had a talent that I never knew about. It turned out there's another *seer* on the island and someplace in our ancestry, we're related."

"So, is it possible that one of the children that appeared on the island could be a *seer*?" asked Raffe.

"I don't see why not, if their heritage goes back to the daughter of a *seer* in a previous generation."

"Not only am I fascinated by the concept of the *seer* but this makes me want to know more about my parents, about where I came from."

Molly squatted on a rock, staring intently, "What are these flowers? They look just like some I've seen in the forest on Morgan's Knot."

Raffe knelt down, "I have no idea what they're called but when you try to pick them, they spray a stinky green mist that smells awful."

"Bet they're the same," said Megan, "but how did they get here if they grow there?"

"The only way they could be growing in both places is if someone or something took them from one place to another," said Kelly.

"But it doesn't necessarily mean they only grow in these two places. They might grow everywhere," said Ian.

"Yeah, but they couldn't be exactly the same this far away. They'd adapt to the new environment," added Morgan.

"We'll have to keep a lookout to see if we find them someplace else," said Josh.

The tribe gathered around a huge bonfire in the middle of the plaza and animals wandered in with their young to join the festivities. It was the first time the ghost children were introduced to the offspring of the creatures of the forest. Bear, lion, and tiger cubs climbed into laps, two young giraffes bent down to lick faces, and baby monkeys cuddled with everyone. Two young elephants carried the smaller children on their backs and the babies wandered among the humans, accepting treats and affection. Tic and Brandy sat with several big cats in deep discussion and Magnus was cozying up to a large owl.

A full moon perched just above the trees to the east and stars filled the dark sky. A gentle breeze rustled through the palm fronds and the silhouette of the pyramid glowed in the darkness.

Adrian turned to Raffe, "You mentioned that your traditions are as they have always been, that it is written. What did you mean?"

"That is what I learned from the older children before they were moved to the underworld."

"Can you read?" inquired Adrian.

"No, although some of the children who were left here by the pirates can. If we had materials to work with, we might learn from them. As you might have noticed, there are children from many different countries. We've all learned at least a little of their languages but most of our conversations are in English."

"Where is it written?"

"I don't know. I learned that our lessons came from the Book of Natural Balance," replied Raffe.

"I'm curious about the pyramid and this ancient city. There are pyramids like this in Egypt and in Central America. The city is almost classical in its construction and arrangement. What's left of the columns reminds me of ancient civilizations in Babylon, Rome, and Greece. What can you tell me?"

"The legend states that, generations ago, the lands to the east were invaded by armies that rose out of the oceans. They had horses, armor, and weapons that were far more advanced than anything the natives possessed. They also carried a new disease that spread like a plague through the local people. The invaders conquered whole civilizations in a very short time. They drove the population from the cities and stole gold and precious stones that they loaded on their ships."

"A group of leaders gathered their sacred texts and sailed away, looking for a safe place to continue their way of life. Evidently, they landed here and constructed this city and the pyramid. No one knows what happened to them or how long they've been gone."

"I'm curious about the pyramid. Have you ever been inside it?"

"No. We believe that it's haunted and avoid it."

"Is there an entrance?"

"I'm not sure but I'll take you there tomorrow."

"I think we might find some of the answers to our questions. Let's go first thing in the morning."

Chapter Seven

It was bright and sunny, as the group trooped along an animal track through the jungle surrounding the pyramid. Adrian remembered studying the construction of the pyramids of Egypt in school. The builders used the stars to line up the structure in very precise angles, which allowed the tombs to function as observatories and calendars. The oldest of the Egyptian pyramids, and those found in Central America, had been constructed to form giant blocks with sloping sides, each tier smaller than the last. A grand staircase climbed the south face with narrower steps at the center of each side and the combined number corresponded to the number of days in the year. Shadows cast across the southern face of the pyramid also predicted the passing of the seasons.

Tic and Brandy led the procession up a narrow path that wound through a dense forest growing around huge stone plinths bearing broken columns at the base of the manmade mountain. Tic stopped in the middle of the trace, "Someone passed along this trail fairly recently. There are broken twigs and branches along the ground that no animal would leave. Brandy and I haven't found any scent but whoever moved through here was moving away from the plaza."

Adrian and Raffe bent down to look at the small sticks and leaves broken from the plants that bordered the path. Tic was right, the leaves were green and the buds on the tips of the tiny branches had not withered. The young *seer* inquired, "You said that you and the other children never go near the pyramid?"

"That's true. We don't come here."

"Interesting. You're sure that there are no other people living on the island?"

"Absolutely, we all know every nook and cranny."

They pushed through the trees to face two fearsome gargoyles guarding the base of the pyramid and stared up at the enormous structure, glowing pink in the sunshine. Stones chiseled and fit precisely into broad stairs, the lips worn and smoothed by the wear of centuries, bounded by a parade of fearsome animals and serpents ascending intricately carved banisters on either side.

Morgan said, "This is amazing! We've seen pictures of pyramids in books but this is even more incredible than I imagined. It's huge!"

Adrian smiled, "I'll bet if you count the steps, the total will be ninety one on each side...plus one at the top will equal three hundred and sixty-five!"

Kelly took Adrian's hand, "Can we climb it?"

"Sure," replied Adrian with a smile. "We might have a better view from the top, but keep your eyes open, I'm looking for a way inside."

The ghost children blended into the jungle that crept up to the base of the pyramid like a lush green carpet but the new children scampered up the steps to the first level, where it formed a broad terrace.

Molly said, "Why don't we walk around the sides to see if there are any entries?"

"Ok," replied Adrian and they set off to the right. The flat surface was inlaid with stones of different colors, in mosaics that formed fish and animals, and arched tunnels bored beneath each staircase. They walked all the way around the formation but found no entry.

Megan, Molly, Ian, and Josh ran ahead to climb the steep stairs, while Morgan, Kelly, Adrian, and Raffe followed a bit more slowly. Adrian kept peering over the sides of the staircase in hopes of finding some hint of a hidden opening.

They continued to the very top, where they found a cap piece with a large red crystal inset in the peak that glowed in the sunshine and large slots carved at the center of each side. Adrian struggled to fit his head into one of the slits. It was too narrow to crawl through but he could see a glitter in the light cascading down into the darkness below.

He pulled his head out of the opening and said, "It's hollow. There's a shaft down inside."

Molly said, "It's too narrow even for Kelly!"

"I'm convinced there's a way inside but it isn't up here." He spotted Magnus circling overhead, "Do you see any way inside?"

The eagle cawed, "It's smooth on all four sides from top to bottom."

They turned to look out over the island. Whoever constructed the monument had been clever enough to place it at a point where it could not be viewed from the sea but with an open view across the little city to the ridgeline that ran like a jagged spine to the southern part of the island. The black conical mountain rose up to the north like a hulking paradigm for the pyramid.

Adrian sat down on the top step and stared out to the south, "Whoever built this liked to line things up in prefect symmetry. They were very precise and nothing was left to chance. The pyramids that were built in the Americas were used for worship and sacrifices to the gods."

Morgan was quiet for a moment and then said, "I remember reading about that and it seems to me that the priests made those occasions very theatrical…with grand entrances and dramatic use of light and shadow. They wanted to produce as much spectacle as possible to awe the worshippers, although, this was not a place for sacrifice. This was built as a monument to life, to nature. These people understood the Balance, so maybe the answer isn't up here. Maybe it's down there."

Kelly pointed to the plaza in the old city, which, because of the genius of the original architects, seemed much closer with the remains of the ancient buildings framing either side of a site line through the single white column standing at the center, "Look, there are arrows pointing at us!"

All of the other children gathered to look down on the ruins of the ancient city and saw that the stones running through the core of the plaza were slightly darker than the surrounding pavement and formed arrows pointing to the pyramid.

Megan smiled and said, "Well, there's the first hint!"

Adrian wondered how the ancient stonemasons carved the stones to form those shapes and then lined them up so perfectly. The only way to align the shapes was to look straight down at the pattern from far above…and, in the days of sailing ships, there was nothing that offered that vantage point. He stared down the stairs and noticed that the shadows, cast by the short walls on either side of the stairway, formed a shape like the undulations of a serpent's body. The head of the snake stopped just short of the level below. "Am I crazy, or does that shadow leading up the steps look like a snake to anyone else?"

Josh and Ian both agreed and bounded down the stairs to jump into the shadow snake's mouth. The other children followed and fanned out across the flat surface of the third level. Tic and Brandy sniffed at the stones around the stairs and the base of the next step. There were designs inlaid into the pavement on each side of the stairway and Brandy kept sniffing at one in the shadows on the left, "Look at this! This one forms a man with his arms extended up in the air and his legs are bent as if he is about to leap and, over here above his head, there are scrapes in the stone."

The children gathered around Brandy to look at the curved marks on the pavement and the figure. Kelly bounced across the body and jumped on the man's stomach. Suddenly, a rumbling echoed from deep within the pyramid, the stones parted and a doorway appeared. Kelly turned around with her best coquettish smile for her companions.

"You've found it," cried Morgan, gathering Kelly up in her arms for a big hug.

"I told you that you'd be valuable on this trip!" cried Adrian.

Kelly blushed bashfully and walked over to peek inside the cleavage in the stones. Adrian reached above her and pulled on the stone door but it would not budge, "Come on everyone, let's see if we can pull it open."

They all heaved and pushed on the stone door and it opened enough for Adrian to peer into a long narrow chamber, beneath the staircase, that stretched to the other side of the pyramid. A pedestal stood at the center, lit by a single shaft of light falling from one of the slots in the peak of the pyramid. On top of the podium was a book with a golden cover.

Tic pushed through the opening and walked slowly to the pedestal, sniffing the air, "There've been humans in here…recently." He leaped up onto the stand and turned back to Adrian, "This looks just like the Book of Wisdoms!"

"Raffe, could you ask your friends to bring up some kind of lever to pry this door open a little more? I think that we've found something very valuable."

Raffe walked over to the center of the staircase and yelled to his companions at the base of the pyramid. They all turned and focused on Raffe. Several of the younger children covered their ears with their hands.

Morgan walked over to Raffe and whispered, "Whoever built this pyramid designed this platform to amplify voices. Try whispering and see if they can hear you."

Raffe said, very quietly, "We need a large, strong lever to move a heavy stone."

The children at the bottom scattered into the forest and returned with a long, thick branch. Several of the older boys struggled to haul it up the steps, followed by the rest of the tribe.

They pushed the branch into the opening and heaved it back and forth until the door moved slightly. They repositioned the branch and tugged again. After several tries, it opened enough for Adrian to squeak through.

He rushed to the podium and stared down at the golden cover of the book. Raffe, Morgan, Ian, Josh, Molly, Megan and Kelly followed. "Tic's right. That looks just like the Book of Wisdoms at the Professor's house!" exclaimed Morgan.

"This must be the Book of Natural Balance," whispered Raffe, touching the cover with two fingers. "Stories of this book have passed from one child to the next for hundreds of years, yet none of us has ever seen it before."

Adrian opened the heavy cover. The familiar figures moved around on the pages and the other children looked on in awe and silence.

Molly leaned to Raffe, "This is one of the ancient texts that we were talking about. Adrian can understand the writings in this book!"

Adrian concentrated on the strange moving figures, "I'll need quiet to do this." The rest of the children backed away.

"Are there adult people living on this island?"

The figures rushed around the page, for several moments, and formed the word "Yes."

"Do they live underground?"

Again, "Yes."

"Is there an entrance to the underground?"

"Yes."

"Where is it?" asked Adrian.

The figures rushed around and around and finally formed a circle. It turned black.

Raffe looked over Adrian's shoulder at the black circle. "That's the pit!"

Adrian asked, "Is that the only entry to the underground?"

The figures formed the word "No."

"Can I gain entrance through the second opening?"

"No."

"Does it allow entry from the underground to the surface?"

"Yes."

"Where is The Crystal?"

The figures moved around and around and finally formed a triangle.

"The Crystal is underneath the pyramid," said Adrian. The children from Morgan's Knot all nodded knowingly.

Raffe asked, "So there is a Crystal on the island?"

"Finding this book pretty well confirms it and we can be sure that your ancestors understood the Powers," replied Adrian, who turned back to the smoky pages. "Is the only entry from the surface to the underground through the pit?"

"Yes."

Adrian paused for a moment and then asked, "Who is the master of this book?"

"Protus."

Adrian smiled, remembering the story that Uncle George told him when he first arrived on Morgan's Knot. Protus was a scribe from Atlantis. Like the maiden Alius and her brothers, he survived the volcanic eruption that demolished the island. The ship that allowed his escape must have traveled through the Atlantic to the Americas. This book survived and was passed from generation to generation. His name, his legend, and his work endured through thousands of years.

He stepped back from the book and noticed a blue crystal glowing gently in the wall above the podium. "Does anyone have any other questions that we should ask of the book at this time?"

Raffe stepped forward. "Ask it if my parents live in the underworld."

Adrian stepped up to the book. "Are Raffe's parents alive?"

"Yes."

"Do they live in the underworld?" Raffe stepped up to look over his shoulder.

"Yes."

Raffe stepped back from the book with weak knees and trembling hands. "It said 'Yes'." Morgan and Molly put their arms around him, as he crumbled to the floor and his eyes filled with tears, mumbling, "I always hoped…"

The children emerged from the hollow space in the pyramid, chattering like magpies with the ghost children, who crowded around the doorway, and marched down the steps, through the forest to the plaza in the ruins of the ancient city.

The ghost children brought food and drink and everyone sat down in the shade. Raffe squatted next to Adrian, "I have to find my parents."

"And I have to rescue mine. They're in the underworld. When can we go?"

"Tonight. I'll have to organize the rest of the children to care for themselves, but now we know that we can get back to the surface, if we have to."

"It's settled, then. We'll go tonight."

"You said that you'd explain The Crystal."

"The brief explanation is that there are pairs of giant Crystals buried in various places across the Earth. In each pair, one Crystal is positive and the other negative and they form a perfect balance. Where we come from, the people have harnessed those powers to provide almost everything they need. Part of the Balance is the harmony between man and nature. The animals are equals and work with the humans to maintain and improve conditions on the island. They're a vital part of our life."

"The people who live there use the powers to provide light and heat, for communication, to power vehicles for transportation around the island, to grow lush crops at a fantastic rate, and to provide healing powers that doctors use to mend the sick. There's a pair of Crystals here on this island and I'd bet that the people living in the underworld are using those powers."

Raffe's mouth was agape with disbelief.

Molly interrupted, "It's true. Most of us grew up there and everything that Adrian's telling you is true."

"I never thought about it before but none of the children on the island has ever been sick. We gather our water from the spring that trickles down from the pond beneath the waterfall. Maybe that's the source for our healing waters," smiled Raffe. "I can't wait to learn more about these crystals. We just accepted the glowing stones that we found in various places around the island like the column and at the top of the pyramid. We've noticed that, at times, they glow and, at other times, they pulse but we've never understood their significance."

"The Crystal beneath the pyramid is the reason that the people who fled the mainland chose this island. They used those powers to build the pyramid, the city, and to provide for their society. I think we'll find some of the answers when we get to the Underworld," said Adrian.

As the last wisp of twilight evaporated above the plaza, Adrian and Raffe stood before the other children, gathered in a large circle around them.

"For the first time, we know that those who have passed to the underworld are alive. We've also learned that there is a way to return from the underworld to the surface. Adrian and I are going to find the truth and I trust that all of you will carry on, as we have for generations, until we return."

"Our new friends are our guests and I trust that you will care for them as you care for each other. They know how to talk with the animals. Learn from them. If the pirates return, you all know what to do. Save the children! I love each of you as a brother or a sister. Have faith in each other and in yourselves. We will return!"

The children all cheered. Kelly ran up to Adrian and wrapped her arms around him. "I'm afraid something will happen to you. Don't go!"

"I have to but I'll come back, I promise," said Adrian, as he leaned down and took Kelly in his arms. "Our ticket home is down there."

Kelly looked into his eyes with tears streaming down her little round cheeks, "Please come back."

"I will."

The fires were lit across the plaza. Raffe was tied to the post on the left, Adrian to the one on the right. All of the children gathered around the two stakes above the pit and reached out to touch or hug the two boys. Molly, Megan, and Morgan made no attempt to hide the tears as they kissed them on the cheeks. Josh and Ian looked worried and wished Adrian and Raffe good luck.

Tic and Brandy trotted up to the boys at the last minute and rubbed against their legs. Tic looked up at Adrian and said, "We'll look after the other children until you get back!"

"Get Magnus to patrol the coasts, just in case those pirates come back."

"We'll take care of it," said Brandy.

Morgan stepped in front of the two boys, her voice quivering, "I don't know the words that you've used in these ceremonies but I have to say that we all pray that you survive and return for us. We all love you."

The crystal on top of the column began to pulse. She walked between the two boys, as the posts groaned, tilted forward, and began to descend into the blackness in the pit.

Chapter Eight

Edward Li relaxed into a plush leather seat, as his private jet streaked across the Pacific. He would land at a small remote airport in western Mexico, where the authorities had been paid handsomely to turn a blind eye to his arrival. He looked forward to meeting with his partners in the Americas. If they agreed to his proposal, a new cartel would take control of the drug trade on the west coast.

His assistant, Michelle, knocked and entered the private cabin. "Jorge is on the line."

"Thank you, I'll take the call here," he replied, reaching for the phone at his side. "Jorge!"

"I'm looking forward to seeing you. Are you on schedule?"

"Yes, we should be there in less than two hours, as we agreed. Is this line secure?"

"Yes, it's encrypted. I'll meet you there. I have transportation set up to check out La Isla de los Ninos. As I told you, it has been the depository for captured children for hundreds of years. It does not appear on any charts and, for some reason, it doesn't show up on radar until you're almost on top of it. I think it's the perfect choice."

"We will make that assessment together. I look forward to our meeting. Is Jake on schedule?" asked Edward, straightening his silk tie.

"Yes, we'll be there when you arrive," laughed Jorge.

"I'll see you then," smiled Edward, dropping the phone into the cradle. Michelle knocked and entered the cabin, carrying a hanging bag with his clothes for the meeting. She turned into the forward cabin and closed the door behind her. Edward removed his coat and tie and changed into jeans, an old cotton hooded sweatshirt, and black high-top Keds. He smiled as he stepped in front of a small mirror and donned the Padres baseball cap that Michelle had, so thoughtfully, included with a pair of mirrored aviator glasses. With two days of stubble, he would appear to be just another worker to any who might be watching.

The sleek jet touched down with a gentle bump on the tarmac at a tiny industrial airport carved in the foothills north of Villa Hidalgo on the western coast of Mexico. Other than the landing lights, the airport was dark and deserted. As soon as the plane taxied off the runway, the ribbon of lamps on the field were extinguished and the jet rolled to a stop inside a large dimly lit hanger at the edge of the field.

Edward Li waited as his assistants secured the plane and checked the hanger for threats. A small "ding" sounded in the cabin to signal that everything was secure and the viceroy could disembark. He stepped through the door into a blast of hot, dry air, instantly reminded of how intense the heat could be in this part of the world, different, certainly, than Hong Kong.

Jorge and Jake emerged from a large black van as he reached the bottom of the stairs. Jorge was from Ecuador but his English was almost perfect. He wore a hot pink Hawaiian shirt, old jeans and flip-flops. His huge black moustache curled with his smile, as he wrapped Edward in a bear hug, "Welcome my friend. It is good to see you. Of course, you know Jake."

Jake, a large muscular eastern European, Romanian perhaps, exuded a menacing air in his very presence. He wore a gray silk suit, open at the collar revealing several chunky gold chains. His dark calculating eyes crinkled into a sly grin as he shook Edward's hand with a surprisingly soft touch, "Welcome back. I believe this will prove to be a profitable endeavor for all of us. Shall we go?"

The three men walked to the black van, its windows mirrored to conceal their presence and the entire body armored against weapons fire or explosives. Jorge's and Edward's armed guards jumped into a second truck and drove out into the night, heading north to a small marina where Jorge kept his racing boats.

"You're sure this island is secure?" inquired Edward.

"It's been used for hundreds of years to stash the children of those who were unfortunate enough to have their boats commandeered by the liberators who plied these waters. It is the pirate code that no child will ever be harmed when a ship is taken but that is not to say that we don't go back to collect them when they've become young adults!"

"I'm sure there's an ample slave market for these children but I would suggest there is more profit to be found in the East," replied Edward with a knowing smile.

"We'll have to explore that possibility," laughed Jorge.

"I've had my people checking the charts and the radar installations along the coast. There seems to be a blind spot surrounding La Isla de los Ninos. It's almost as if it's invisible to their surveillance," said Jake quietly.

"I know it'll prove to be the perfect spot to offload our cargos for trans-shipment to the mainland. It won't be long, you'll see."

"I hope you're right. By design, we seek the path of least resistance," replied Edward.

After thirty minutes, the van rolled to a stop beside a pier in a ramshackle marina. Jorge led the two men along the quay to his newest acquisition, the Tigger2, docked across the end of the gangway, her engines rumbling quietly. The deckhand jumped off the boat and untied the lines, while the guests found their places, "She's fueled and ready to run. Have a safe trip."

"Gracias," replied Jorge, as he took the wheel and gunned the powerful engines, "This is my latest liberation, the fastest boat on these waters. Even the Coast Guard can't catch this one."

The powerful racer slipped away from the dock and idled to the mouth of the cove, where Jorge eased the throttles forward. The boat jumped to speed and arced to the northwest.

Edward leaned forward and asked, "How far is the island?"

"It'll take about forty minutes to get there. Jake, why don't you get us some drinks from the bar down below? It's well stocked!"

Jake disappeared and returned with three glasses and the finest malt Scotch in a crystal decanter. The three men talked of their plans in the luxury of the smooth ride. Presently, Jorge throttled back the engines and the boat eased to a crawl.

The island loomed out of the darkness and Jake idled past the jagged rim of the south end of the ridge, knifing into the water like some serrated war ax, cleaving waves that scoured north along each coast. He motored west along the rocky shoreline for a few minutes before the boat slowed and he aimed the beam of a searchlight through a narrow gap into a sheltered cove.

The snug entry opened to a secluded and protected bay surrounded by sheer slabs of rock. There was plenty of room for six or eight custom fitted racing craft to maneuver comfortably and the power of the sea etched a deep rock shelf, several feet above the high watermark, more than a hundred yards around the back of the cove. It would provide ample space for the temporary storage of their cargo.

Jorge turned on his depth finder, "It says that it's twenty two feet. That should be more than enough."

Edward Li smiled, "It is as you promised it would be and more. I'm impressed. Our ships can stay in the safety of international waters and we can run the cigarette boats from here. I would suggest bringing in a supply of fuel."

"I've already started working on that. We have a large trawler that's being outfitted with tanks. It will carry enough fuel for many trips between the ships and the mainland."

Jake inquired, "When will your first shipment arrive?"

"Can you have everything ready in a week?"

Jake and Jorge smiled and raised their glasses to toast their new business alliance.

"Yesterday, we hijacked a Nineteen-Forty-One, fifty-seven foot, Elco yacht. A classic cruiser in mahogany and cherry, only seven of

84

them ever built," said Jorge. "Stupid trust-fund baby and his pals tried to resist. Now that beauty's all busted up and it's gotta go in for repairs. It's not right to spoil something so beautiful. But, on the flipside, we captured two primo blond coeds who'll fetch enough for the bodywork from the slavers and, today, we celebrate a bright future for our new enterprise!"

"If we all deliver on our promises," said Edward Li, "we'll all prosper handsomely."

Jorge turned the boat slowly to allow the searchlights to scan the sheer vertical cliffs jutting out of the water like ragged teeth. They did not notice the small pyramid carved into the rock at the top of the bluff with a small red crystal pulsing rhythmically.

The boys stared straight down, lashed to poles that creaked and scraped into perpetual night. "Good luck," called Adrian.

"I sure hope you know what we're doing!" replied Raffe with a nervous laugh.

The echoing voices of the children on the plaza faded and the boys were blind to each other and the bottom of the pit. The gearing behind the posts groaned and quaked and, for a moment, Adrian wondered about the logic of his plan but the answers to their questions lay at the bottom and there was no turning back.

"Does this ever end?" yelled Raffe.

"I sure hope so!"

Presently, a faint red glow appeared in the distance and the rhythm of footsteps echoed up the shaft.

The posts swiveled upright in an ancient cavern carved out of volcanic rock. A very old man with a long flowing beard, dressed in deep blue robes, appeared out of the darkness. He stared at the two boys with the most perplexed look, "This is highly unusual! You have been taught to send mature people into the pit. Neither of you is an adult!"

The boys looked at each other and struggled to free themselves from their bondage. Finally, the old man walked behind them and untied the ropes that secured them. "Please follow me," he said curtly, turning abruptly to stride down a narrow tunnel.

Red *orbs* cast enough light to follow the old man, who moved with surprising speed along the channel. The boys trotted to keep up and eventually the tunnel opened through a lock into a huge room with a glass domed ceiling restraining the ocean above.

The old man walked over to another man and a woman, also dressed in deep blue robes, as the boys gazed around in wonder. The new man looked very stern, "You've broken a covenant that has existed for hundreds of years. No child has ever descended into the pit and, in your case, there can be no return! What do you have to say for yourselves?"

The two boys glanced at each other, like school boys caught in a prank...standing before the headmaster. Adrian cleared his throat and said, "We've come to save our parents."

"You parents are safe. You'll be reunited presently. You two have confounded a system that has functioned flawlessly for centuries. I'm not sure what to do with you!"

"Well, you could take me to my parents and you could introduce Raffe to his!" replied Adrian, defiantly.

The man scoffed and looked at his companions. "You leave us little choice. Please follow me."

He pressed a panel next to a lock on the far side of the room that spiraled open into a glass tunnel. The boys peered around in awe, the creatures of the sea were swimming over and around the passageway in swarms, illuminated by *orbs* on the outside of the structure. A reef encased the base of a second glass sphere, home to sharks, barracuda, rays, and every variety and color of fish. Schools of glittering silver flitted in and out of the corals. Fans and sea grasses waved seductively in the flow of the currents and two divers, dressed in strange gray suits, shrouded in shimmering silver bubbles, zoomed under the corridor.

They passed through another lock into a smaller glass dome. Adrian looked up to spy George, Ponte, Travis and his parents standing a few feet from the access and ran into his mother's arms. He released one hand to hug his father, just to be sure that they were both alive. "I'm so glad that you're safe!"

"I know and I wish we could have let you know what happened to us but you were already on your way here and Dadeus had no idea where to send a message until Ponte arrived!"

Adrian hugged his Father and then George, Ponte, and Travis one by one. He turned to introduce Raffe, who was still standing near the door to the tunnel and seemed stuck in place, too timid to walk the few steps to the smiling couple, frozen with their arms outstretched to their son.

"Raffe," said Sara, standing, "I'd like you to meet your parents, Morag and Jim."

The other couple stepped forward and enveloped Raffe in a long and loving hug. Raffe was in tears, "I understand why we have to save the children who are left on the island by the pirates but how could you give me up?"

His father looked down into his eyes and said, "My son, I am so very proud of all that you have accomplished on the surface. You learned to survive and to lead. You've cared for countless children and taught them to be self-sufficient. If we'd raised you here, you'd never have mastered those lessons."

His mother said, "This system was invented to protect the older children and to allow the younger children to learn to live within the harmonies of nature. Giving you up was the hardest thing that either of us has ever done but it was the right thing to do at the time. Both of you have much to learn about our history and our future. There will be time for that now."

Raffe's parents walked to the far side of the room with their arms around their son, a moment for privacy and reunion.

Adrian turned back to his parents and fell into a human knot, with everyone's arms wrapped around him, a warm secure blanket, lost since his parents sailed away from Morgan's Knot on the Sparrow.

"George and Ponte have been telling us about your adventures and your bravery on the island. We left you there because we thought you'd be safe while we sailed the boat around. We had no idea that you were a *seer* or that you would be forced to grow up so fast! I'm very proud of you," said John, smiling with pride. Adrian felt that his father treating him as something more than a boy for the first time.

George interrupted, "Once again, you've come to our rescue!" Everyone laughed.

Ponte stepped up, "I have so many things to show you! All of our discoveries pale in comparison to the technology that these people have developed. It's fascinating!"

Adrian hugged the old man and turned to Travis and George, "I'm so glad that you're alright. We watched the Jasmine disappear and you with it!"

"Well, we're both fine. The Jasmine is docked in the interface not far from here. As Ponte said, their technology is rather amazing."

The three people, who escorted them to this room, returned. The woman called to them, "Everyone, please join us. We have much to discuss."

Raffe and his parents walked over to the group who were taking seats on a long sofa that curled out of the glass like a question mark around a low round table rising out of the smooth stone floor. The woman pulled the cowl from her head to reveal a soft glowing face surrounded by a mane of mahogany tresses. She had Adrian's blue eyes, a small straight nose, and full red lips. "I am Mary. This is Dadeus, indicating the man to her right, the Keeper of the Powers." Other than his eyelashes and bushy eyebrows, he was completely bald. "This is Gabrielle, our leader."

Gabrielle, the man with the flowing white beard, moved to stand in front of the small group, "Raffe, I understand your feelings about being left on the surface when you were very young. This custom evolved generations ago when it was realized that the children who grew up on the island taught each other to live in harmony with nature and to survive on their own. By the time the young adults are sent to the underground, they have matured beyond their years and are far more valuable in our undersea world."

"This tradition was started as a defense against the pirates, who plundered this island until all the adults disappeared, deposited what they couldn't handle, then returned to collect those children who had matured for sale into slavery…or worse. In the same way, the tradition of the children covering themselves in ashes grew from the pirate's superstitions about ghosts. They viewed the gray children as the living dead and left them alone. This deception was invented by the children without knowledge of the reason for the effect, it just worked."

"Certainly, we've developed technologies that could keep the pirates from ever finding this island again but our society is built on generations of kidnapped children. The pirates continue hijacking boats from the unprepared, so we've continued with our traditions through these many generations. Although our system is unusual, it has produced an endless stream of brave and independent adults. We have dedicated our lives to saving people who have been shipwrecked or seized by pirates and our primary goal has been to save the children of these hijackings."

"Raffe, you've lived on the surface for years and you've always known that there were lions and tigers and all sorts of animals living in the forest who could have taken a child whenever they felt hungry. Do you remember any child who was lost?"

Raffe thought for a moment. "No, the children were never attacked by the animals, although we taught each other to be afraid of them."

"The animals are part of the harmony or the Balance, as they call it on Morgan's Knot. They were there to teach you and to protect you.

We live in equilibrium with the creatures of the sea. They are our friends and our allies."

Raffe smiled, "I'm just beginning to learn about The Balance. Adrian and his friends talk with the animals."

"Well, in spite of Adrian and his friends upsetting these traditions that have been carried on for so many years, I think that everyone on the surface will benefit from their lessons."

Adrian and Raffe glanced at each other struggling to contain a grin. Raffe's parents sat on either side of him, arms wrapped around his shoulders.

Gabrielle continued, "You are here and we can't send you back. There is much for each of you to learn about our world and, after you've had some time to spend with your parents, you will begin your training."

Just then, another man in blue robes rushed into the room. "Sir, we have recorded a rather unusual breach of security in the cove!"

"Put it up on the screen, we have no secrets here," said Gabrielle.

The man walked over to a glowing circle on the wall and punched in a code. A hologram displayed the Tigger2 slowly turning around and around in the cove, a bright spotlight glittering across cliffs. The voices of the men on board were surprisingly clear and left no doubt about their plans.

Raffe was mesmerized by the image floating in mid-air. He reached out to touch it and his hand passed right through the vision. He turned to Adrian with a look of wonder.

Dadeus turned to the man in the blue robes, "Erin, have the divers attach a tracking crystal to that boat before they leave the cove."

"Yes, Sir," snapped Erin, as he rushed from the room.

Gabrielle sat down with a look of deep concern. "Our system has worked for hundreds of years but the world of piracy has changed. Where they once wanted the ships and the bounty, now they want the means to transport their drugs with impunity. We must find a way to scare them off and put an end to any future plans they might have for this island."

Adrian looked up at his uncle George, who winked. The young *seer* stood, "Sir, I can't pretend to understand your technologies or your history. The fact that Professor Ponte is impressed is enough to make me want to learn everything I can from you. We managed to overcome a similar situation on Morgan's Knot, recently, and I think that by combining our knowledge, we might find a way to frustrate the bad guys."

"Your world is astonishing and I wasn't raised with the same concerns that all of you were, but it seems to me that, if we're going to take on the pirates, perhaps we should find a way to change your system so that no child born on this island should ever again be separated from their parents." He paused for a moment and added, "And while we're at it, we should create a plan that will put an end to piracy in these waters once and for all time."

"My boy, your Uncle, the Professor, and Travis told me a little of what you went through to save the island of Morgan's Knot. You have my respect and I'd be more than willing to listen to what you have to say. From what we've just heard, we have one week to create and execute a plan. I'd say we have much to do."

Chapter Nine

Dadeus, Gabrielle, and Mary guided a tour through the undersea facilities. Glass tunnels tethered great caverns, hollowed beneath the mountain, to domed pavilions that erupted from the seafloor like a string of glittering soap bubbles. Although sunlight flooded the undersea city, the spaces were lit with red and amber *orbs*. Mary explained that the *orbs* balanced the color to match daylight because water filters the warm tones.

The first pavilion was dedicated to private apartments, kitchens, and classrooms. Adrian inquired, "How many people live in this complex?"

Gabrielle replied, "We have more than six hundred people living here and there are sixty-seven children on the surface, if we count your friends."

Raffe asked, "How many of those children are like me, native to the island?"

Mary studied him with a kind smile, "There are twenty-eight, including you."

"How old are they, when you send them to the surface?" asked Adrian.

"Three or four. We want them to be mobile and to have a basic mastery of language before they leave."

Adrian interrupted, "Do you have a *seer?*"

Mary smiled, "Yes, I am the *seer* and we are hoping that Raffe has inherited my talents because Morag is my sister. He'll be taking the test as soon as we can arrange it. We watched you reading from the Book of Natural Balance. From what George and Ponte told me, you learned very quickly. You ask the right questions."

"Thank you," smiled Adrian. "I have good teachers and it wouldn't surprise me to find that Raffe is a *seer*. He seemed to understand the figures in the Book, while I was reading about his parents. I have another question. The Book said there was another entrance from the underworld to the surface. Where is it and do people from the underworld visit the surface?"

"There is a passage that we use to move back and forth. It is behind the waterfall above the pond in the forest. There's another that opens from the pyramid but it is rarely used. I have to admit that I did sneak out the other night when Professor Ponte was cast into the pit. Your arrival was most unusual. To answer your question, yes, we do move about on the surface when the pirates come to the island to hunt for children and when there is an emergency."

Raffe gasped, "The ghost people! Many of the children have caught glimpses of you over the years but, by the time we could investigate, you were gone!"

"We call those close encounters," laughed Mary. "We also monitor the activities on the surface. You might have noticed the crystals that are installed all over the island?"

"I always wondered about the glowing crystals. Sometimes they glow and at other times the seem to pulse."

Dadeus smiled, "They're programmed to serve several functions. They act as cameras to allow us to watch the activities on the surface and as microphones so that we can hear what is being said. They are also hooked together in a series that allows us to send and receive information through the vectors, to monitor the surrounding oceans, and to activate weather patterns, as necessary…sort of a crystal antenna."

"Is there a negative Crystal?"

"Yes, there's a Black Crystal several miles off shore, between the island and the mainland."

Adrian looked at Ponte, "And is there a third crystal?"

Dadeus looked inquisitive, "A third crystal?"

"Yes, we found that there's a third crystal balancing the positive and the negative. On Morgan's Knot, it was close to the Black Crystal.

Nanchez is working on its function and properties but we haven't found the key to understanding it," replied Ponte. "Adrian learned about it when he entered our Crystal. It was the key to regaining control during the storm."

Dadeus pondered these revelations for a moment, "Well, in that way, you're ahead of us. We've always assumed that the two Crystals balanced each other. What you're saying is that there's a third Crystal that is the key to that equilibrium?"

"Yes," replied Adrian and Ponte, at the same time.

Dadeus smiled, "There is always more to learn about the magic of the Crystals."

The group moved into the next dome, where large ducts extended out into the ocean. "This is our food processing center. We harvest the plankton and tiny creatures of the sea to make most of our food. It is highly nutritious and, as you will see, we've developed many ways to make delicious meals," said Mary. "We also grow and harvest plants on the ocean floor in much the same way farmers raise crops."

The whole room echoed with a deep whooshing sound, as water and nutrients rushed through the pipes. Gabrielle added, "We process seawater into fresh water, which we use for drinking and personal uses, as well as for our industrial processes. The fresh water is broken down into oxygen and hydrogen, as well as the other components. It also allows us to create fresh air, which is safer than trying to conceal intakes on the surface."

They exited through another lock, along a tunnel, and into a chamber that opened to the ocean. Adrian's ears popped when the seal on the door to the passageway closed. The Jasmine was tied to a walkway and looked to be in perfect condition. Several other boats and small ships were also moored in the vast cavern.

Across the dome a portal opened to the sea, yet water did not flow into the breach. Adrian looked inquiringly at Gabrielle, who smiled. "You'll have noticed a slight pressure difference, when we entered this chamber?"

"Yes, my ears popped when you closed the door," said Adrian.

"The pressure in this section is just slightly higher than the pressure of the water, so it stays outside the bounds of the compartment."

Adrian gazed around the gigantic dome. Along one side, a series of frosted glass doors glowed electric blue. Two divers emerged dressed in wet suits that were iridescent gray with large black, upside down teardrop shapes over their eyes.

Adrian turned to Dadeus, who had been in quiet consultation with Ponte, "I noticed your divers moving through the water at a fairly incredible speed and they seemed to be surrounded by long bubbles.

Dadeus smiled, "You are very observant, young man. Our divers use a technology that encapsulates them in a thin film of air. We've found that when the bubbles move through water, there is no resistance. It is as if the air is slippery to the water. This allows our divers to move along at high speed without making any noise or disturbance in the fluid. A small breathing apparatus is incorporated beneath their goggles, so they can travel long distances without having to stop to renew their air. Their suits are also equipped with communication devices that allow them to talk with us and each other."

"I'd love to try that!"

"Oh, you will. Both of you will begin training tomorrow," smiled Dadeus, who turned back to his quiet consultation with Ponte.

After passing through several other domes, they returned to a dry cavern that had been excavated deep beneath the mountain to expose a giant red Crystal, spinning a few feet above the floor. "This looks familiar!"

The Professor and Dadeus were roused from their whispered conversation. Ponte laughed, "Yes, this is very much like our Crystal, with a slightly different composition. This one is based on rubies."

Adrian replied, "Well, I might have guessed that from the color!"

"Yes, but our friends have developed systems that go far beyond anything we have. For instance, I have been in contact with Nanchez through the vectors that extend out across the globe."

"This system allows us to monitor the movements in the ocean for hundreds of miles in every direction. We are also capable, on a small scale, of generating almost any weather pattern that we might need. The storm that came up, before the Jasmine disappeared, was generated from the next room," added Dadeus. "We created a vortex in the ocean that allowed us to lower the trawler into a bubble, where our divers and submersible craft could move it about under water without damage to the craft or the people on board. Unfortunately, when your parents' boat was caught in the storm, we were couldn't reach them before the craft was shattered and they were set adrift. Mother Nature's fury is far more powerful than anything we could create."

Travis laughed, "That's all well and good, if you know what's happening, but I'm afraid our perspective was a bit more frightening!"

Dadeus patted him on the back and smiled, "I'm sorry we scared you but we couldn't leave you out there for all the world to see on their radars!"

Gabrielle took the two boys aside, "This is the short tour of our facilities. There is much more that you will learn about our world over the next few days. I'd suggest that we enjoy a meal together and rest for the night. Each of you should spend some time with your parents. I'll be interested in your suggestions about how we can foil the plans of these drug smugglers and, at the same time, stop their piracy."

The boys looked at each other and smiled. "We'll have our thoughts organized by morning and we're ready to help in any way we can," said Raffe.

After dinner, Adrian followed his parents to their private apartment. He was enthralled by the view through a large glass shield that opened to the sea and fish swimming past in the glow of the *orbs*.

He pulled himself away from the panorama and turned to his parents, "I was about to climb the mountain to replace the balancing crystal when we found out that you were missing. I guess I have Aunt Elsie to thank for calming me down enough to make the right decision but I was so worried about you."

"George and Ponte told us the story last night and, to tell you the truth, I couldn't believe what you've been through. We assumed that you were just a normal boy who would spend a few months safely enjoying a very magical place. In hindsight, I might have suspected that you were a *seer*," said his mother, gripping his hand as if she would never let go again.

"You'll never know how hard it was for us to leave you on Morgan's Knot but, as it turned out, it was the right decision on many levels," smiled his father. "I am very proud of you."

"Thank you. I just did what had to be done and you would have done the same things. That's what you taught me."

His father stared at him, "We taught you to be a good and responsible person but you far exceeded anything we might have expected. You showed true courage when you had every reason to turn away from that challenge, not once but twice."

"From what we're hearing from Ponte, the two sides have merged together and are making considerable progress towards improving life on the island for everyone. Elsie and Shannon have established that you and Alius are very distant cousins," said his mother.

"We wondered about that. We have so many features that are similar. She's a beautiful girl with a very strong spirit. She almost killed me and I her. I guess that tangle will tie us together forever."

"I was most impressed with how you organized the animals to help. I wish I could have been there to see that menagerie," laughed his mother.

"Well, I didn't really organize them, Tic did. He is one very special cat and I hope he's doing the same thing for the children on this island. Brandy has a very big heart. He led me through the blizzard to the Knot and the balancing crystal. I knocked myself out in a fall and was ready to give up but he kept going. I learned a lot from him."

His father interrupted, "I think we should all get some sleep. Tomorrow is going to be a long day. We've just started learning about this place and training with their divers. It's exciting and totally exhausting, as you'll learn tomorrow."

Adrian climbed into bed with a kiss and hug from each of his parents for the first time in months, a warm glow he only felt when they were together as a family.

They turned out the light and Adrian gazed up through the glass ceiling at the sea creatures glittering the wash of the *orbs* outside. Although he was tired, he let his mind wander back to Morgan's Knot and the lessons that he learned during his two trips up the mountain. *"I can adapt those lessons to solve the problem that we're facing here,"* he thought, as he drifted off to sleep.

Adrian awoke to bright, shimmering light cascading down through the ocean above the complex. It was truly beautiful. *"It's the animals and the weather. Those are our tools,"* he thought. *"And those diving suits sure look like the drawings that people have used to describe aliens...maybe we can make the pirates believe that they're battling aliens! Someone said the pirates are superstitious, we should work with that idea."*

He bounded out of bed to find his parents already dressed. He put on a blue robe and followed them down to the dining hall, where they enjoyed a breakfast that seemed surprisingly normal, considering it was all made of plankton and tiny sea creatures.

Raffe and his parents joined them at their table. The new *seer* sat down next to Adrian, "Have you any ideas?"

"Yes, I have a rough scheme going in my head but it'll take an incredible amount of organization and at least one of us is going to have to go back to the island to work with the other children."

"You realize that the pirates have automatic weapons and aren't afraid to use them?"

"We have the powers of The Crystal, the systems that your people have developed, all of the children on the surface, and we have the animals. We just have to figure out how to neutralize their weapons. Remember, I've done this before!"

Raffe laughed, "I've spent my whole life being responsible for the other children. This is the first chance that I've ever had the opportunity to participate in an adventure!"

Adrian leaned over and whispered, "How'd it go with your parents?"

Raffe was quiet for a moment, "They're far more special than I might have hoped. We talked for a long time last night and I understand why this system exists but I'd rather have grown up with them, if I'd been given the choice."

"Look at it this way, you've learned many things from your life on the surface. They'll serve you well and, I would guess, prove to be of great value in this battle we're facing. Besides, if we do this correctly, no other children will ever have to be separated from their parents again. And I know we can win."

Raffe blushed, "I'll do whatever we need to do to bring the children together with their parents and the lost children to this world."

Mary escorted Adrian and Raffe to the access dome, where she introduced Soule and Amy, "We call this sphere the Interface, because it's our entry to the sea. Soule and Amy are master divers and they'll be instructing you for your first lesson with the bubble suits."

Everyone shook hands and Soule said, "We've heard a lot about you two and we're looking forward to teaching you how to fly through the water. Amy has found two suits, which ought to fit. You'll be scanned this afternoon to measure you for your own second skin. You can change in the dressing room, behind the frosted glass doors, and I'll show you how to put them on."

Soule opened a translucent panel into a small room where they removed their robes and sandals and donned the bubble suits, which were snug and completely gray. A stiff webbing flowed back from the wrist into a fin at the elbow and the feet extended into flippers like a frog. Amy was waiting with two headpieces when they returned to the platform in the Interface, "I assume you both swim?"

Both of the boys nodded, as she handed each a helmet. "Before you put these on, there are several things that you must understand about our system. Inside the helmet, you'll find a soft seal that fits around your nose and mouth so you can breathe without a mouthpiece like the old scuba gear. The eye patches enhance your vision and compensate for the density of the water. You can also talk with other divers and the command center."

"It's fairly normal for new students to breathe rapidly when they first enter the water. You'll have a moment of panic until your body and your mind realize that air is flowing in and out and it's not going to quit. Just take slow deep breaths and you'll be fine."

"If you look at your left wrist, you'll find a watch implanted in the material. It is also a timer, a depth gauge, and a compass, which are not only useful but, occasionally, life-savers. On your right wrist is a panel of tabs to direct your communications."

Soule added, "Once we're in the water, the air bubble will form automatically. It provides propulsion for rapid movement through the sea. You move forward by stretching your body out and pulling your arms to your sides. To slow and stop, simply move your arms away from your body. The hardest thing for new divers to learn is to avoid making sharp turns. The air bubble has a hard time maintaining a fluid shape, when twisted in a radical turn, so make your turns slowly and smoothly. Try to look out ahead and decide where you're going before you get there." He grinned, "The best part is that the sensation is almost like flying."

"Do you have any questions?" asked Amy.

The two boys beamed at the thought of flying through the water, "What happens when you stop?" asked Adrian.

"The air bubble that surrounds your body shrinks to a thin film that clings to your wetsuit like silver jelly. Don't worry, you'll still be able to breathe normally. Just remember to think ahead and make your movements slowly. The object of our exercise today will be to teach you to glide through the water gracefully, to stop, and then return to speed."

The boys pulled the helmets over their heads and Soule secured the seals around their necks.

Adrian marveled at an extraordinarily clear vision of Raffe and smirked, "You look like an alien!"

Raffe laughed, his voice had a crisp electronic pitch through the headphones, "I don't know what an alien is…is it good or bad?"

Adrian crackled, "Some people believe they've had encounters with creatures from another planet and their descriptions resemble these wetsuits!"

The four divers clumped down a shallow ramp and Adrian looked down as he placed his foot in the water, a gleaming bubble formed around it. He leaned forward to place his face in the water and tried breathing. At first, he gasped for air but forced himself to take several deep breaths and his panic faded.

Soule moved next to Raffe and glided slowly through the entrance to the open sea. Amy coasted alongside Adrian, her gentle voice filled the inside of his headpiece, "Keep your arms away from your body a little. We don't want to move too fast through this chamber. Once we're out in the open water, we'll speed up. Try to stay beside me and follow my lead."

They drifted out through the aperture beneath the dome and accelerating slowly. Amy's voice crackled through the headset, "Slowly pull your arms to your sides and aim straight ahead."

Adrian pulled his arms in and shot through the sea like the dolphins, Spot and Dusty, in the dark waters of the North Atlantic around Morgan's Knot. The air bubble formed a second skin insulating his suit from actually touching the water. They were right, the sensation of zooming along felt very much like flying…or, at least, his dreams of flying! He wanted to do flips and rolls but Amy was just inches from his right side.

"Okay, now we'll try a gentle turn to the left. Just roll your body very slowly and you'll begin to turn."

Adrian leaned left and felt his direction change. He pulled his arms tightly to his sides and gained more speed.

Amy's voice appeared inside his head, "Very good, now, let's try turning to the right."

Adrian arced to the right, his body soaring through the water without effort, and he yearned to go faster.

"Okay, now let's try to stop. Pull your arms away from your body very slowly and let your legs fall underneath you. You don't want to come to an abrupt stop."

Adrian extended his arms away from his sides to strong resistance, like fins pushing against the fluid. His motion slowed and he allowed his feet to dangle. Amy floated around in front, "We're neutrally buoyant, so you'll stay at this level. You can make yourself rise by taking in a deep breath or you can descend by exhaling. If you breathe normally, you'll remain relatively stable."

Adrian took in a deep breath and his body started to rise. Amy reached out and grabbed his arm, "Now exhale!"

He let out his breath and slowly descended to face her again.

"I think you're beginning to get this! Let's go for a fast run and we'll make some slalom turns. Adrian pulled his arms in to his sides and zoomed through the water on Amy's starboard flank. "Now bank gently to the left and then to the right."

The student tore after his mentor and only guide back to dry land, first left, then right, skimming along through daggers of sunlight just beneath waves on the surface, then straight down to glide just above a reef climbing a long branch of craggy rocks, defiant remnants of an ancient eruption extending the roots of the island like fingers under the seabed.

Adrian looked around, fascinated by dense flowing schools of colorful fish swimming through the sea fans and grasses that grew around the masses of coral. Urchins hobbled along on long stiff spines and lobster and crab scurried from one protected pocket to another, searching for a meal. He reached out to touch a yellow fish that brushed against his glove and could not help but think, *"This is magic."*

Amy's voice bubbled in his headset, her enthusiasm infectious, "That's a long-nosed butterfly fish. Isn't the color incredible?"

"It's amazing! What about that black one with the thin yellow stripes?"

"That's an imperial angelfish and just beyond it is a queen angelfish. See the blue one over there, that's a blue tang, and there near the bottom, that large guy who's sort of loping along, that's a grouper."

They spent a few minutes cruising along the reef. Amy slowed and stopped before a large formation with many holes, "Most of the sea creatures are friendly but a few have an attitude. Remember, we're aliens invading their turf and they have every right to defend it. If you look closely, you can see the pattern of a Green Moray eel hiding in this hole. He's not friendly, so don't try to touch him or even disturb him. Your suit will protect you from most of the things that might attack but don't push it. Don't touch anything unless you know what it is and you have a reason to investigate it."

"This is fantastic!" cried Adrian.

"We all have the same reaction. Every time I get to go out into the water, I learn something new about our propulsion system or about this amazing world and the creatures that live here. I don't think that anyone ever learns it all." Adrian could feel her smile, even though her face was hidden inside the strange headpiece with sad eyes. "I think we should start heading back to the dome. You've done very well for your first lesson!"

They raced across the sands, sunlight and shadows dancing from the surface, and slowed at the interface. Adrian was entranced by the complex stretching to many domes on either side with connecting tunnels between the main structures that glowed like warm luminous spheres in the blue-green of the water

The divers climbed the ramp to the platform and Soule and Amy pulled off their helmets then unfastened the seals around the boys' suits to remove the headpieces. Their hair wasn't even wet.

The boys could not contain their smiles. "That was so much fun!" exclaimed Raffe, "I'm ready to go again!"

Soule grinned, "You'll have plenty of opportunities to practice. We'll go again tomorrow, if that's alright with you."

"You bet," said Adrian. They returned to the dressing room, changed into the blue robes that everyone seemed to wear, and rejoined their instructors on the platform.

"I believe you're to meet with Gabrielle and Mary in the residential dome. They'll be waiting for you," instructed Amy. "We'll see you in the morning."

Raffe said, "Thanks. We'll be ready."

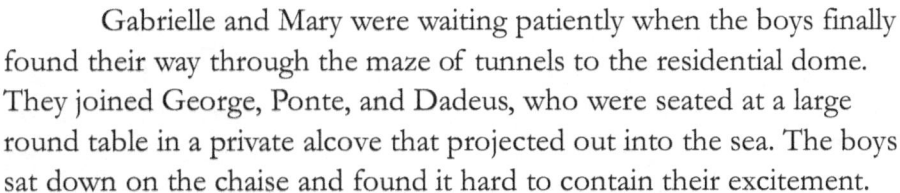

Gabrielle and Mary were waiting patiently when the boys finally found their way through the maze of tunnels to the residential dome. They joined George, Ponte, and Dadeus, who were seated at a large round table in a private alcove that projected out into the sea. The boys sat down on the chaise and found it hard to contain their excitement.

"From your expressions, I might assume that you enjoyed your first lesson," said Mary with a knowing grin. "We all feel that way, even after years in the ocean."

Raffe smiled, "It really does feel like flying through the water. I always felt envious of birds that could fly so high they disappeared, somehow that always seemed to be the most complete freedom that any living creature could have. I guess I'll have to add fish to my list!"

Everyone laughed before Gabrielle spoke, "Ponte and George have been telling us a little more about the storm and your heroics on Morgan's Knot, Adrian. Although I must remain skeptical, I am open to your suggestions. Do you have a strategy to diffuse our current predicament?"

Adrian paused to gather his thoughts, "I've been thinking about the pirates and their plans. First, you said that they're terribly superstitious. Perhaps we can use that against them but, before I go on, I have a few questions."

"As Ponte might have told you, the disruption of the third Crystal on Morgan's Knot led to an incredible storm. I watched the squall you created around the Jasmine and was wondering, how large a storm can you produce?"

Dadeus replied, "We could easily surround the entire island with a miniature hurricane, if we needed to. What you couldn't see when we plucked the Jasmine into hiding was the calm in the middle of that downpour. From Travis' point of view, he was surrounded by a storm that had no effect on the boat."

"My second question is how big an object could you move through the water and how far could you move it?"

Dadeus was quiet for a moment, "Well, we've moved several fairly large ships out of harm's way, when hurricanes were approaching. I would have to have additional information to calculate an accurate response to your question."

"How about a freighter?"

"That's a large vessel. How far would you want to move it?"

"To San Diego."

"San Diego? That's more than two hundred miles up the coast. We've never tried to move anything that big that far. It would tax our entire power system. Why San Diego?"

"When my parents left Morgan's Knot, I spent some time studying the maps of their route and noticed that there's a large naval base in San Diego. I wonder what they would do if a boatload of drugs bobbed up in the middle of their harbor?"

Everyone laughed.

"So my question remains, could you move a freighter that far?" asked Adrian.

"Before I give you an answer to your question, I'll have to do some calculations."

"Okay. It seems to me that we have a bunch of things working in our favor. We have the fact that the pirates are superstitious and they don't know the terrain of the island or that we're preparing for their arrival. As far as they know, the Island of the Children is inhabited by children. We have a network of observation Crystals on the surface. We might have the power to move their boats and ships over fairly long distances. We have a small army of children, who the pirates have sworn not to harm, and we have the animals," said Adrian.

"On the other side," he continued, "They have automatic weapons and we have to believe that they wouldn't hesitate to use them to protect themselves or their cargo."

Adrian stopped for a moment to allow Raffe and the adults to consider his observations. He continued, "When we invaded the *others'* tunnels, we based our plan on the idea that, if we adhered to a belief in The Balance, no human being or animal would die by our efforts. As far as we know, a few of their guards were injured in the scuffle with the animals but no one was killed in the battle."

Again, the group nodded their understanding. After a few moments Gabrielle spoke, "I think I see where you're going with all this. You're suggesting that, perhaps, we can scare them away?"

Raffe added, "They seem to believe that the children they've seen on the island are ghosts. Perhaps we could expand that to include the animals."

Adrian smiled, "I knew I liked you!"

Gabrielle raised a hand, "So, your plan is to organize a small army of defenseless children and a herd of wild animals to frighten these...thugs...into submission in the next few days? That hardly seems possible."

"On the contrary," replied Ponte, quietly. "He's right on point. None of the adults in the underground have any fighting experience and, if they showed their pale faces on the surface, the pirates would not hesitate to break out the heavy artillery and destroy everything you've created over hundreds of years. His plan offers the only alternative to direct confrontation and massive loss of life on both sides."

George added, "I know it's hard to believe but these children rallied herds of farm and forest animals into a disciplined militia that succeeded in invading the enemy's lair which was guarded by well-armed professional soldiers. We had no weapons, let alone organized defenses, so without them, we would have lost everything."

Gabrielle stroked his beard, "Then let us pursue this avenue of thought until we find a better alternative."

"There is no better solution," said Adrian. "This is plan A and B rolled into one and there isn't going to be a second chance."

"None of us is going to come up with anything as imaginative or as likely to succeed as Adrian's plan," said Mary, "and we don't have the time or the resources to prepare two strategies in the next few days."

"I have to agree with you, my dear," replied the old man. "We've survived on a steady influx of independent children but I find it hard to burden them with the responsibility for the future of our entire culture. We could hide them until the pirates have done their business, if all else fails."

"But that doesn't accomplish anything," argued Adrian. "If you want to be done with the threat once and for all, this is your best chance. Take it or leave it."

The old man smiled but his eyes bored into the boy's spirit, "Whether youthful arrogance or innocent genius, we have no other options. We will proceed as you suggest."

Everyone started talking at once and paid no attention as Ponte and Dadeus slipped from the room. Twenty minutes later, they returned.

Dadeus looked very serious, "We've done some calculations and I don't think that we have the power to move a vessel that large over that distance."

Adrian asked, "What if you combined the power of the two Crystals?"

Ponte responded, "On Morgan's Knot, we learned that the third Crystal balanced the other two."

Dadeus replied, staring at Adrian with a curious expression, "We don't know where the third Crystal is on this island, let alone how to control it."

"I know what you are thinking," said Adrian, turning to the Professor. "We both know where to find the answer, although I'm not sure that I want to try that again!"

"That's up to you, my boy, but I doubt whether the books can provide the technical information we'll need to generate enough power to accomplish the final piece of your plan."

Everyone turned to Adrian, who stared at the glassy reflections on the table and pondered his encounters with the Golden Crystal. He survived the ordeal twice and gained valuable knowledge but an ominous little voice in the back of his mind kept singing, *"...the third time's the charm..."*

The young *seer* stood beneath the giant Red Crystal in a cavern in the very foundations of the pyramid, surrounded by his parents, Raffe, Ponte, George, Travis, Gabrielle, Dadeus, and Mary. The air swirled about the room as Dadeus shouted over the din, "No one has ever attempted anything like this with this Crystal. From what Ponte told me, this is somewhat larger than the Crystal on Morgan's Knot. Are you sure that you want to go through with this?"

"Each time I've entered a Crystal, I've admitted that we had no other choice and I believe that to be true again." He was overwhelmed by the frightening magnetic attraction pouring from the gigantic gemstone whirling above him. He withdrew the golden key from his pocket and held it up to his Mother, "You told me that this key would open doors of understanding but you had no idea of which doors I would have to open."

She opened her mouth to say something but the rush of wind drowned out her words.

He turned back to the Crystal, wiped a small dune of red gems from the smooth stone floor to reveal a familiar slot. He inserted the key and a booming voice bellowed, "Who seeks entry?"

"I am Adrian and I am a *seer*!"

"We shall see," said the voice.

Adrian turned for one last look at the crowd in the cavern, Raffe and Mary put their hands over their ears, his father held his mother, who buried a knuckle between her teeth, and the rest stared awestruck. The enormous red gemstone rotated faster and faster. A dark hole appeared and he stepped through the breach onto a tiny circle and, again, felt as if he was bound, like a bug waiting for liquid amber to solidify around his body, inside giant glass tornado. The familiar figures marched around the glittering interior of the Crystal at a faster pace than in the Golden stone on Morgan's Knot. In the flash of reflection on his last encounter, the figures moved away through the swirling blaze of ruby radiance and a globe appeared. One giant landmass broke into pieces floating across the sphere, bits and pieces crashing one into the next, driving mountains into the sky and carving great seas between the continents. Red and black lights appeared here and there and, as a young Earth turned, some were extinguished. Finally, the globe stopped, with single pair of red and black dots glimmered over that patch of Pacific where La Isla de los Ninos rose from the sea.

As Dadeus indicated, the Red Crystal appeared under the mountain and the Black Crystal several miles offshore. The booming voice returned, "You are a *seer*! How may we assist you?"

"I am curious about the third crystal. The balancing crystal."

"This island was created by a vent beneath the ocean that erupted to form the volcano and carried these Crystals, from their birth in the molten core during cataclysmic collisions, to the surface. Over time, the plates moved off the vent, sealed the flow of magma, and crashed into the fragment that hangs like a tail to the south. Eventually, another atoll will appear to the southeast of this island. In that turmoil, the third crystal was moved and now resides deep in a tunnel that leads from the ocean beneath the land. It opens below the sheltered cove on the west side of the island."

"Is there any way to replace that third crystal to combine the power generated by the Red and the Black Crystals?"

The voice was silent, as if considering every possibility, "There is but disrupting the circuits would be very dangerous. The balance between the two primary Crystals might be lost forever."

"I understand, as I've had a similar experience with the Golden Crystal on Morgan's Knot. In that situation, we removed the third Crystal to stop the flow of power between the two primary Crystals. We replaced the third Crystal and the power was restored. During the interruption, we accomplished our mission."

"You are attempting to merge the power from these Crystals, that is a dangerous process."

"Is it possible?"

"Yes."

"How would I accomplish this task and how long would I have to replace the third Crystal without damaging the other two?" asked Adrian.

The voice was quiet and Adrian could feel his energy draining away.

"The balancing Crystal is blue. You would have to replace it with a Golden Crystal but you must return the Blue Crystal within one hour. To wait any longer would mean the annihilation of the Crystals and this island in a cataclysm unmatched since the crust of the Earth cooled. The power created would be several times greater than the energy being generated at the moment and it will overwhelm the systems that have been installed on the island. Your Keepers must use extreme caution in balancing the two opposing forces by alternating the currents to achieve maximum energy with the best hope of safety. They must be in phase with each other, if they are not, the power will cancel itself out and short circuit the Crystals."

"Is there anything else that I should know?"

"This task can only be accomplished by a *seer* and it might command the ultimate price."

"Thank you for your instructions. I'll follow them exactly and I will not fail."

The figures marched across the ruby rush in front of Adrian's face and the dark hole appeared on his right. He turned and stepped through the gap to find everyone standing in exactly the same positions as when he entered the Crystal. Fiery streaks of light swept around the cavern and he collapsed in a puddle of rubies.

Chapter Ten

Adrian opened his eyes and realized that he was completely naked, immersed in a bath of warm ocean water. He was breathing normally, although no hoses were attached to his nose or mouth, and his body felt completely rested and revived. He had no idea how he had been transported from the swirling interior of the giant Red Crystal to this strange wet environment. His eyes slowly focused on his parents staring down through ripples on the surface of the liquid.

He sat up, sputtered, and coughed up a fountain of water. His mother wiped his face with a warm towel. "You gave us quite a worry," she said, her tired eyes strained and sad. "I realize why you had to enter the Crystal…but please don't do that again!"

"Believe me, each time I've done this, I hoped it would be the last," said Adrian as he stood up slowly and dried himself.

Gabrielle helped him into a chair and checked his pulse. He held up a tiny *orb* and scanned Adrian's eyes, "How do you feel?"

His father handed him blue robes and he pulled them over his head.

"Considering the fact that I fell out of the Red Crystal and awoke immersed in a tank of water, surprisingly well. Thank you."

"Well, this is not ordinary water. It is highly oxygenated and there is a tiny current pulsing through the fluid to boost your immune system and your energy level," smiled Gabrielle. "We've found this therapy useful in the treatment of many ailments. After all, our ancient ancestors evolved from the sea and our composition is surprisingly similar to sea water."

"I know where the third Crystal is located. It's in a tunnel under the cove and it's blue. The Crystal told me that we can combine the energies of the two primary Crystals by substituting a Golden Crystal. It also said that you should alternate the currents in phase with each other but the increase in power would probably blow out your wiring. If we decide to use it, you'll probably have to shut down the power to most of the underworld and increase the capacity of the circuits that will control the movement of the freighter. We'll only have one hour to execute our plan or the Crystals will be destroyed."

Gabrielle stared at him with a quizzical look on his face. "So it's true that the Crystal talks to the *seer*? Had I not seen it myself, I would never have believed it possible."

"Yes, it feels like a discussion, although I'm not sure that anyone was really talking. The voice isn't just all around you, it's inside your body, your mind."

"Remarkable. We watched you enter the Crystal, in absolute amazement, and, almost instantly, you reappeared and collapsed. We thought you were dead but Ponte and George assured us that you would recover."

"It's a strange sensation. I could feel the energy draining from my body but I couldn't stop the conversation until I learned how the process works. I think I should give up this habit," smiled Adrian. "I'm not sure how many times my body will recuperate!"

Sara reached into her pocket and held out her hand. She opened her fingers to reveal the golden key, "You've used this more wisely than I might have imagined. Keep it with you."

Adrian smiled, took the key, and dropped it into the pocket of his robes. "I am never without it and I'll need it again when I change out the Blue Crystal."

His mother looked worried, "Why must *you* change the Crystals?"

"Only a *seer* can change the Crystals."

"Mary is a *seer*."

"I know but I've done this before. I know the steps."

Gabrielle smiled patiently, "We're testing Raffe, as we speak. It is possible that we have three *seers* in our midst."

Adrian was delighted, "I knew it!"

Gabrielle continued, "I'd suggest that you get some rest. You'll continue your training in the morning and then we would like to meet to discuss our plan. There is much to do and little time to accomplish everything that needs to be done before the pirates return."

Adrian thanked Gabrielle for reviving him. His body felt as if he had a good night's sleep but his mind was exhausted. He followed his parents out of the clinic and through the tunnels to the apartment in the residential dome.

As they settled in, his father sat down beside him, "I honestly don't believe what we just witnessed. You've grown in so many ways, since we left you on Morgan's Knot. You've shown bravery and wisdom far beyond anything I might have expected of you. I just want you to know that I'm very proud of you." He put his arms around Adrian and held him close.

His mother sat down next to them, "I think I've been holding my breath since you entered the Crystal. I couldn't believe what you were doing as you stepped into that spinning monster without hesitation. My poor brain didn't believe what my eyes were seeing."

"I know. The first time, on Morgan's Knot, I was positive those jagged crystals would just carve me into little pieces. Ponte told me that he'd only seen it done once before, when Justus had to enter it. If there were an easier way to find out what we need to know, I'd definitely choose the alternative!"

Sara put her arms around her husband and her son, "You might still be a boy but you are a very brave man in my eyes."

They found Raffe and his parents in the dining room the next morning and the new *seer* could not conceal the broad grin on his face.

"You are a *seer*!" cried Adrian.

"I am!" replied Raffe. "I was wondering whether you might help me learn about this special talent?"

"I'd be happy to help. When I learned that I was a *seer*, Tic told me that it involved a huge responsibility. I didn't understand what he meant until I was asked to do things that were far beyond my experience and my worst nightmares too. Understand that it's not what other people expect of you but rather what you expect of yourself."

Raffe's smile vanished, "I'm ready to learn."

After breakfast, the boys returned to the interface, where they found Soule and Amy waiting. They changed into their new wetsuits in the locker room behind the blue glass panels and joined their teachers in the dome.

Amy said, "I understand that you had quite an evening. Are you feeling strong enough for another lesson?"

Adrian smiled, "Gabrielle tried to drown me in the clinic but I'm feeling much better today!"

Soule and Amy laughed, "After talking to Gabrielle, I understand that they have determined that Raffe is a *seer* and that you'll need some special training to enter a tunnel. Do you know which of you will be volunteered for this task?"

"No, at this point either of us could do it. I think that decision will depend on the rest of our plan," said Adrian.

"I could do it," injected Raffe.

"Well, maybe we should train both of you, so there are more options when the time comes. We'll need these *orbs*, in addition to the floodlights on your helmets for detail work," she said, holding up several amber *orbs*. These attach to your left forearm, behind the gauge, which will leave your hands free to work."

The boys put on their helmets and fastened the lamps to a scratchy patch on their left sleeves. The four divers padded down the incline into the water and swam through the entrance to the sea. Adrian, entranced by the shimmering air bubble that stretched out like a silver cocoon, drew his arms to his sides to slip through the water. He noticed other divers working around the residential dome, some manning strange bulbous craft to move heavy beams. The submarine machines looked like glass globes with large, powerful pinchers that held and manipulated cargo and tools. Red and amber *orbs,* mounted on top of the clear spheres and the adjacent domes traced two of the craft moving an enormous beam in perfect unison while two others waited to position the girder in a cluster of arches to support the next sphere. Adrian spoke into the microphone inside his headpiece, "Are those the craft that you used to move the Jasmine?"

Soule's voice crackled in his headphones, "Yes, they're a wonderful invention. They're capable of very delicate work, like placing those beams and the bolts that tie them in place, but they also morph into long slender torpedoes to move through the water at incredible speeds, much faster than divers in these bubbles, even when they're carrying heavy loads."

The four divers fanned out and sped north to the entrance of a narrow tunnel that disappeared into the black heart of the volcano. Soule's voice erupted in Adrian's headset, "Turn on your *orbs* and follow me. Stay close and don't touch any living creature unless you clear it with one of us. There are some unfriendly critters that hang out in caves and crevices."

The boys lit their *orbs* and followed Soule into the mouth of the cave, checking every crack and crevice for sea creatures waiting in ambush. Amy brought up the rear. The sides of the narrow channel were jet black and light from the *orbs* reflected shiny crevices, glistening like amber spider webs, as they dove under the mountain.

Amy's voice whispered, "Are either of you claustrophobic?"

Raffe replied nervously, "A little!"

"Does this situation bother you?"

"Yeah, but I'm okay."

"Will you be able to work on your own under these conditions?"

"I'll be nervous but I know I can do this, so let's go!"

They reached a chasm slightly wider than the tunnel that offered space to face each other. Raffe floated up, bouncing on the ceiling of the tunnel. Amy's voice whispered through the headsets, "Quit holding your breath. Breathe normally."

Raffe sank back down to face his companions.

"This tunnel was once used as an conduit for power cables. The cables were held in place with these large pins that you see anchored into the walls of this little fissure. The pegs are tapered and beveled on two sides. They only fit in the hole one way and they'll stick if they're not inserted exactly perpendicular to the plate. I want each of you to remove and replace the pins smoothly. There are four on each side, Raffe you take the left and Adrian the right. Remember, it's harder to move gracefully in these tight quarters, so take your time and concentrate."

The boys moved to face the walls of the tunnel, the four protruding pins glistened in the light of their *orbs*. Each was firmly planted into a plate in the stone, the shank splayed as if a large spike was pounded into a too small socket, cleaving the excess steel into ringlets that curled back on the peg. They offered only a ring to grasp and required considerable strength to extract from their sockets but more dexterity to replace them in a smooth motion while trying to remain neutrally buoyant. After several tries, the boys were removing and replacing the pins with fluid movements and they did not seem inhibited by the confining conditions.

"Okay, both of you seem to have this down! How does it feel?"

"No problem," replied Adrian.

"I think that I can do this without worrying about the tight conditions," said Raffe.

"The big problem will be when you have to wait for almost an hour and then go through the reverse process," said Adrian.

"I'll be alright," replied Raffe. "I know I can do this if I have to."

Amy's voice came through again, "You've both passed this assessment. I suggest we go around to the other side of the island to check out the tunnel where you'll be working."

"Let's go!"

They swam back through the dark channel and zoomed off to the north. The two boys flew through the water, giggling with the freedom of flying through the ocean at the speed of a falcon in the air. Two dolphins, Dee and Slate, joined the quartet and moved into formation beside the two boys. Adrian wanted to reach out to touch their new companions but he knew that extending his arms would reduce his speed.

They rounded the north shore and headed south along the west coast to the cove, where they found a hollow at the entrance to the bay and explored either side. On the right, a narrow crevice cleaved into the rock. Soule moved to the front, "Let me go first. Occasionally, we find sharks sleeping in these tunnels and they don't like being disturbed. Stay a few body-lengths behind me until we reach the end."

They swam single-file into the darkness. Their *orbs* glistened on the craggy stonewalls so narrow they couldn't see beyond the diver in front. Soule slowed to a stop as the narrow tunnel expanded into an open chamber and pointed to a faint blue glow in the far wall of the dark cave, "Is this what we're looking for?"

Adrian swam up to the blue light, fanned the sand away, "This is it. We don't want to touch anything but let me show Raffe how this works."

Raffe moved closer and Adrian pointed to the glowing Blue Crystal. There were four amber crystals surrounding it. "This is the primary Crystal. To remove it, you have to insert my key in this slot," he said, as he brushed silt away from the rock beneath the Crystals, revealing the keyhole. "Push these four crystals in the order north-south-east-west…The Crystal will rise up in it's mount. After you replace it, you have to push the side crystals in reverse order. Basically, take the Blue Crystal out, replace it with a Golden Crystal for a little less than an hour and then reverse the operation. I think that north is to our left, so that's the first one you'd push…and west would be the last. Then remove your key. There is one more thing. This can only be done by a *seer* and the *seer* must be alone."

Raffe peered down at the cluster of crystals, "I can do this, no problem."

"How about having to hang out in here for an hour? The bubbles insulate your body to a point but your temperature will drop and you won't have much room to move around in here. I'd guess that, when you're that cold and tired, replacing the original crystal will be much more difficult than extracting it," said Amy.

"I can do this, I promise!"

"The power will increase as soon as the golden crystal is drawn back down into the mount, so you'll have to time the replacement exactly. Win, lose, or draw, I'd say fifty-nine minutes. No matter what happens you can't let it to go beyond one hour."

"Got it," replied Raffe.

"Okay, let's get out of here!" said Soule.

As they swam out, Raffe inspected the walls of the cave and felt more assured that there were no deep pockets where large creatures could hide. If there was a shark in here the next time he entered, they would meet face to face.

Darkness gave way to the light of the open sea and Adrian asked, "How about our communications? Will the system work between the domes and the tunnel?"

Soule replied, "It's a closed system, so we should be able to communicate but I'm not sure what will happen when Dadeus shuts down the rest of the grid to accommodate the increase in power. We'll have to talk with him about that."

Dee & Slate cruised into formation, as the divers swam around the south end of the island and up the east coast to the interface. Slow to climb the ramp to the platform, all four were exhausted.

As they pulled off their helmets, Soule said, "This is going to be a difficult mission, even for an experienced diver. You'll be working alone in a dark, tight environment and you'll have to be patient enough to stay put for an hour, no matter what happens. Are you both sure you're really prepared to do this?"

The two boys glanced at each other, "Yeah, I think that either of us is capable but let's make sure that we can talk with each other. Whoever isn't doing this will have to direct the children and the animals and we'll want to synchronize everything. It'd be great if we could talk between the surface and the tunnel."

"We'll have to coordinate that through Dadeus," said Amy, who walked over to a panel on the wall and spoke into a *messenger*. "They are expecting you in the residential dome."

The elders were waiting for the divers in the meeting room. They had already started lunch and the boys were famished.

Mary said, "I understand that your training is going very well. At this point, the consensus seems to be that we'll need one of you on the surface and the other in the tunnel. Ponte and Dadeus want me to stay with them through this process, in case there is a need for the insights and references in the Book of Natural Balance when they transfer the power system."

Gabrielle continued, "We've been exploring the various possibilities and there is one that we haven't discussed with you. That is that the pirates have not been back to the island in several years looking for mature children. We would not be surprised if they didn't use this opportunity to scout the island."

"They've never figured out why there are no mature children but they continue to search for them on a fairly regular basis. Greed for the profits of the slave trade, I would guess," said Dadeus.

Raffe injected, "We've been talking about that too and agree that one of us should work with the children and the animals and the other in the tunnel. Our concern is that we'll need to be able to communicate with you and with each other. If you have to change the circuitry for the increase in power, will the communications system still work?"

Dadeus and Ponte both spoke at the same time. Everyone laughed. George smiled, "You two are like two children with a brand new toy!"

Ponte responded, "Well, we each knows part of the magic of The Crystals and we're learning from each other and from Nanchez on Morgan's Knot but there is much to discover in short order."

"The crystals that are installed on the surface act like an antenna, in that they transmit and receive. They're our means of primary control over communication, surveillance, moving objects around in the sea, and projecting squalls. To answer your question, we're hoping that the communications system will be functioning normally. We're working on the balance between maintaining critical systems and I'm hoping that we'll find a solution quickly. In the meantime, we've got an army of technicians reinforcing the circuits."

"We've been watching the children on the surface and they seem to be fine for the moment, but one of you will have to return to begin organizing their defenses. Until this is over, as you suggested, we would rather not put adults on the surface. If we fail, the pirates will still believe that the island is inhabited by children. If we succeed, well, we'll deal with that when the time comes. Have you two decided which of you will be on the surface?" asked George.

"Raffe has volunteered to replace The Blue Crystal and I'll work with the children and the animals, if that's alright with all of you?" replied Adrian.

Everyone agreed. The discussion continued for several hours before they retired for the evening.

Morgan's hand was tingling with Kelly's elbow wedged into her arm. Ian and Josh were still snoring but the other children were starting to move around in the cave and Molly and Megan were stoking the fire.

Morgan walked over to the fire pit and crouched down next to the twins, "I wish we knew what was happening. It's been four days since we sent Adrian and Raffe into the pit. I hope they're okay."

Molly smiled, "After all that Adrian went through on Morgan's Knot, I'm sure he's alright. I just wish they could communicate with us!"

Megan laughed, "Maybe we should go yell at the Book!"

They giggled together and followed the other girls into the jungle to gather nuts and fruits for breakfast. The new children were beginning to gain a basic knowledge of the wonders and plenty in the forest and respect for the organization and hierarchy that allowed the ghost children to live comfortably without the supervision of adults. The girls were responsible for gathering food from the forest. Groups of boys left each morning to scout the island and the horizon for intruders. Until their introduction to the animals, they hunted for small game. Now they brought whatever they found growing in the high fields to contribute to the communal dinner.

Everyone respected the opinions and ideas of the others and the older children taught their charges to swim in the ocean and to move through the forest without making a sound or leaving a trace, to find food and fresh water, to blend into the jungle when pirates or intruders approached, and, ultimately, to survive. Everyone could predict the weather by the shape and direction of the clouds the sky and the taste of the wind. Each could find their way in complete darkness through their knowledge of secrets of the island and the movement of the stars. History and social lessons were passed through stories shared every night around a fire on the plaza. Ian and Josh decided that, if these children could live in perfect harmony with each other, then perhaps the rulers of the adult world could learn something from them.

Since Tic introduced the animals to the gathering in the plaza, they mingled with the children and escorted the boys on their reconnaissance missions. It was not uncommon for a lion to wander into the cave and settle down next to one of the smaller children for the night or a giraffe to steal a piece of fruit from someone's plate.

Elephants, zebras, horses, and ponies knelt down to allow children to climb on their backs for a ride and monkeys joined in the games played each afternoon on the square.

Every day was filled with chores, games, and a communal sense that they all belonged together. Todd and Sandy were the newest members of the family and the rest of the children were very sensitive to their loss. None of the rescued children knew whether their parents were alive or dead but each held a secret hope that someday they would come back to find them. The other children tried not to mention that no parents ever returned for children kidnapped by pirates and that was something that Todd and Sandy would accept over time.

Josh and Ian left camp with Blackbeard and Timothy, the tiger, to scout the south end of the island. They climbed peaks along the ridgeline to check the beaches and scan the horizon. Occasionally, a ship or a large private yacht might pass in the distance but, other than the pirates, few craft ever approached. The scouting missions were a daily vigil to spot intruders before they reached the island and to warn the rest of the children. Three other groups were patrolling the coastline.

They slipped through the forest to the waterfall cascading into the crystal clear pool, then down through the rocks to a stream that passed into the plumbing system in the ruins of the ancient city. The two boys were about to jump into the cool water, when Josh grabbed Ian's arm and pulled him back, pointing to the shadow silhouetted behind the tumbling sheet of water.

The gray figure was moving. It stepped through the sparkling curtain and turned to stare down at them. It was completely gray, with strange dark eyes that looked like upside down teardrops. There was no nose or mouth and the boys were leaning to run when a familiar voice called out, "Hey guys, what's happening?"

The alien reached up and released the mask, revealing Adrian's smiling face.

"I don't believe it! We knew you'd come back…but we never expected you to look like this!" cried Ian. "What's with the suit?"

"It's a diving suit. You'll get your chance to try this out soon enough. In the meantime, we have much to do. The pirates are coming back in two days and we have to prepare the other children and the animals."

The boys hugged and turned back down the path to the ancient city. Timothy, sleek and nimble, trotted ahead and Blackbeard climbed a tree to swing from one branch to the next with amazing agility, screeching and squawking.

"So, tell us about the underground! Did you find your parents? And Ponte and George and Travis?"

"Yes, they're all well. The underworld is a wonderland, a city beneath the sea, and the people who live there interact with the ocean in much the same way that we cooperate with the animals on Morgan's Knot. Their technology is much more sophisticated than anything we have at home. This helmet has a communications system inside and the suit creates a bubble in the water that allows you to zoom along at high speeds."

"If I didn't know you so well, I'd think that you're teasing us," said Ian.

"No, it's true. I'll explain it all when we get back to the cave. We're going to need everyone to help with our plan."

Half the group was out harvesting food for dinner, while the rest were still on patrol, when the boys emerged from the jungle onto the smooth stones of the plaza in the ancient city. Adrian peeled off his wetsuit and found a loincloth in the cave. Kelly, Morgan, Molly, and Megan followed Brandy and Tic out of the forest and ran to smother Adrian in a hug.

"I knew you'd come back," squealed Kelly.

"I promised I wouldn't leave you," said Adrian.

"We were worried and frustrated that we had no way of communicating with you to find out what was going on!" said Molly.

"More than you know. I'll explain it all when the rest of the children return. It's a long story but the important part is that the pirates are going to return the day after tomorrow and we have to be ready."

"How do you know that they're coming back?" asked Morgan.

"The people who live in the underworld monitor the island and the ocean. A pirate boat was in the cove the other night."

"Magnus saw a boat in the cove but it took off to the southeast right after he found it," said Megan.

"I watched them and listened to their conversation. They have plans to use the island to offload drugs and launch delivery boats to the coast. We're going to stop them."

"How are we going to stop them?" asked Kelly.

"With magic!"

Kelly giggled, "Can I help?"

"Of course, except this time I think you'll have a leading role."

Todd and Sandy ran out of the forest to the group on the plaza ahead of the rest of the tribe and everyone wanted to hug Adrian. Food was prepared and the tribe sat down together in the shade of the palms along the west edge of the square, surrounded by an incredible menagerie mingling with the children and accepted bits of their meals.

Adrian stood up, "My friends, I'm back from the underworld. It's a wonderland beneath the sea and the adults who live there have been watching over you. They send their regards to all of you and we'll all be together in a few days. Raffe has a task that only he can accomplish, so he had to stay with the adults for the moment. In the meantime, the pirates are coming back."

Murmurs and concerned looks dashed through the crowd.

"We have a plan and I hope that, if we're successful, the pirates will leave this island forever and the children and the adults will be reunited."

The children cheered. The animals growled, squawked, snorted, and squealed much louder than the children.

"Are you willing to take on the pirates?"

"Yes!"
"Then we have much to do."

Chapter Eleven

Four cigarette boats streaked west across the Pacific to La Isle de los Ninos. The wind was calm and the boats moved in formation, painting parallel wakes, glistening silver ribbons tracing across long blue-green swells rolling in from the west.

Jorge, piloting the lead craft, turned to Jake, "We'll drop most of the men on the east side of the island while we go on to meet with Edward on the mother ship."

"Why are you leaving the men on this side of the island?" shouted Jake, above the growl of the engines.

"It's the pirates' custom to retrieve mature children from the island. They're worth a small fortune to the slavers…and I'm sure we can find one who would make a nice gift for Edward to take back to the Orient with him."

Jake smiled. The work of pirates might have evolved with the times but the traditions remained unchanged over centuries, "I thought you were sworn to avoid hurting any child."

"We are…but those who have matured into young adults are fair game!"

"I guess you know your business. I'm only interested in delivering our product to the coast for distribution. Our customers are anxious to trade dollars for ecstasy and we must strive to fulfill their expectations. The rest of it is of no interest to me."

Jorge laughed and turned the boat into a long curve to the north, along the east coast, then slowed the Tigger 2 to an idle and steered the beautiful craft towards the beach.

"The pilots of the boats will run around the island to the cove, where they'll wait until after our conference with our friend on the mother ship. The rest of you will march across the island and search for any children who have managed to grow up. Leave your weapons in the boats. We don't want any of the children harmed. There will be a prize for the most beautiful young lady!"

The crew cheered and laughed, as they jumped into the shallow water and waded in to the beach. They whooped and waved as the boats turned south and accelerated across the water.

"Have you been on a raid before?" asked Bernie, a small, squat man with a gray beard.

"No, but this should be fun," replied Thimble, named by Jorge because a hat in the shape of a sewing thimble would fit snugly on his bald head.

"Just remember, we don't harm the children. Capture the mature ones without hurting them. They'll be worth more if they're healthy and unmarked!"

"Have you ever caught any?"

"Well, no, but this time's the charm!"

A large shadow blocked the sun and Bernie looked up, "What is that bird?"

Thimble shaded his eyes, "It looks like an eagle but it's all gray."

"What's an eagle doing way out here?"

Magnus was almost hovering in the gentle breeze and let out a long menacing screech.

"I don't know but I don't like it."

The men marched up the beach and slashed through the scrub at the edge of the jungle on the dunes. On a protruding rock, just above the beach, a red crystal pulsed softly.

They hacked a path into a small clearing in the forest, where they heard a loud growl from the underbrush to their right.

"What was that?" sputtered Thimble, his eyes wide in panic.

"Oh, that's just one the animals that lives in the forest. There's an old story about a bunch of dumb pirates who hijacked a ship carrying circus animals. They didn't know what to do with the critters, so they dumped the whole lot on this island. Sort of like the carnie version of the cavalcade on Noah's Ark!"

Thimble was not relieved. Another low growl rumbled from the shadows on their left. He was following close behind Bernie, looking over his shoulder, bumping the older man and stepping on his heels.

"Watch where you're going!"

"Sorry, I just…I was just trying to make sure nothing was sneaking up behind us!"

"Relax. We should begin to see children, once we've climbed this next hill. Keep your eyes open."

The forest was hushed, save the clumsy crunch of the pirates' footsteps. Birds and monkeys sat in branches above their heads silent and still. They simply watched and flitted from one limb to the next as the group of men moved past. Their course was communicated to the children by other birds and monkeys who passed visual cues throughout the forest.

The pirates charged along a path through the trees and up a hill that overlooked a narrow gorge before another steep rise, more a rampaging herd than a stealthy raid to capture young people in the forest. Two young children stood on the opposite ridge wearing loincloths, their hair and skin completely gray, like statues carved in dark marble, unmoving and defiant, staring at Bernie and the rest of the men. Thimble pointed to the children, "There they are, the ghost children!"

"I guess some of the children that we leave on the island must die. The ghosts won't bother you. They just appear and then disappear."

"I don't like ghosts," replied Thimble. His lower lip was quivering.

"Oh, stop it. They're ghost children, nothing more. You're a bloody pirate! Act like one!"

Suddenly, a lion, atop a large rock up the ridge to their left, growled deep and slow. He was completely gray, just like the ghost children.

"I suppose that that's a ghost lion?" screamed Thimble.

The huge cat turned and disappeared. "Well, some of the animals might have died too. Let's keep going, the cove isn't too far, even if we don't find any youngsters worth the trouble."

They turned back to the path but the ghost children had vanished. The trail twisted down through the trees until it opened into a small clearing at the head of a slender basin between the hills.

A loud screech echoed across the little valley as a gray Magnus tucked his wings and dropped out of the sky at attack speed, his talons extended as he swooped low over the panicked pirates. The men crouched defensively as a line of ghost children materialized on the ridge. Interspersed among the children were all sorts of animals...lions, tigers, an elephant, a giraffe, bears, horses, ponies, zebra, sheep, gazelle, and several dogs. They were all gray and they were staring silently down the hill at the men in the clearing. Magnus' piercing caw shattering the stillness and they all started howling.

The pirates turned to flee up the hill ahead but another column of gray children and animals appeared. The ghosts roared with an explosive din that sent the men scurrying along the valley floor, desperate to find an escape. A horde of wild boar, dogs, fox, and wolves fell in behind the pirates, barking and snarling viciously. The children and the animals closed behind their quarry with a deafening racket.

"This is like herding sheep," said Morgan to Todd, stifling a giggle, as they moved along the ridge.

Tic raced along the peak, meowing orders to the other animals. At the end of the little valley, Brandy led lions, tigers, and bears in a charge on the frightened bandits, driving them through a narrow gap to their right into another gorge. A group of cheetahs, panthers, and two elephants with gray children on their backs were waiting on the next hill to the left and the terrified men were turned up a long, steep climb to the cliffs above the cove.

Thimble was panting hard as he struggled through a patch of brambles. There were ghost children and animals throughout the jungle, herds charging behind them and more waiting on the next ridgeline,

130

roaring the wail of the dead. Snakes, rats, mice, and giant lizards scurried and slithered across the path, while flies, bees, and mosquitoes swarmed about their faces. "How many children did you leave on this island?"

Bernie's face was bright red and sweat was running down his forehead into his eyes, "We didn't leave all these kids. There're others working this coast, maybe they left them here, or maybe they're just multiplying! All the pirates in these waters know this island and live by the code."

"I don't know which scares me more, these animals and children or what Jorge will do to us when he finds out about all of this!" moaned Thimble, as he swung his hands wildly around his face swatting insects clustering on his eyelashes.

Ponte and Dadeus sat before a console directing the power and communications for the island. Blocks of *orbs* blinked across the panel and two screens displayed a video feed from the cove next to a view tracing the progress of the Tigger 2, as it approached the freighter. They checked and re-checked their calculations. The new cabling was in place and the internal circuits would be shut down before Raffe exchanged the Crystals in the cave. All of the power would be channeled through the crystal network on the surface to form a squall, which would create the vortex to swallow the freighter and move it up the coast. A squad of divers and the fastest of their submersible craft were already in place.

Preparations were underway in the residential dome for welcoming the children and Gabrielle had convened a council to determine how to merge life above and below the surface of the island. Someone suggested they consider rebuilding the ancient city to its original splendor and George volunteered to teach the basics of farming using the vectors to accelerate the process.

Every one of the sea people hoped that this quest of the children would allow them to escape a social system that existed for hundreds of years, an arrangement established by their ancestors to protect their children as well as those of the people who had been overtaken by pirates. An unspoken tension in the air exposed the conflicting hopes and fears that tore at the fabric of every heart in the complex.

The residents of the underworld gathered around holograms projected in each dome. The plan was presented to the entire group. Parents, who sent their children to the surface, were torn between concern for their safety and the desperate hope that this campaign would end piracy in these waters and allow them to be reunited.

George and Travis were sitting in the residential dome with John and Sara. Adrian's mother grasped John's hand and her knuckles were white, "I know this has to run its course but I wish we could help."

George turned to his sister-in-law with a confident smile, "Your son came up with a great plan. He's done this before and, in both cases on Morgan's Knot, he was successful. He's a very special young man."

Sara sighed and tried to relax, "I know but, no matter how old they are, they're still babies to their mothers."

John squeezed her hand, "It will all be over soon enough."

Travis chuckled, "I wish you could have been on the island the night he rescued Ester. The fireworks were spectacular!"

They all laughed nervously together.

"I wish I could have been there for my son."

"He's a wise man in a young boy's body," said George, "and he'll become a talented *seer* someday. He has the ability to see the proper path through murky obstructions and he doesn't choose the easy course. This plan is typical of the way his mind works. It was designed to scare but not harm the pirates. The children will never actually be near the pirates, so they should be safe...and his idea of moving the freighter shows a bit of dark humor. If all of this works, the ghosts and aliens of La Isla de los Ninos should be legendary for years to come."

John and Sara stole a glance, "I know you're right, you guided him through those campaigns on Morgan's Knot, but this is like watching your child go to war on television! The hardest part of this is going to come when Dadeus and Ponte shut down the power inside the complex. The holograms will disappear until Raffe replaces the Blue Crystal. We won't know what's happening."

"I know exactly how you're feeling," said George with sympathy and a kiss on the forehead. "I felt the same way when I let him climb the mountain, alone, in the middle of a blizzard. There was no other choice but to let him go. I was absolutely panicked for hours until he came stumbling down the path surrounded by the most amazing collection of animals you could imagine."

"It's probably good that I wasn't there. I wouldn't have let him go!" cried Sara with an anxious laugh.

Suddenly, the hologram flickered and disappeared. The lights in the domes dimmed and fading sunlight, cascading down through the sea, skittered across the room like thousands of flickering golden pixies. A hush rolled through the compound, as if everyone was holding their breath until the lights came back on.

Raffe heard the whine of the engines of three powerful boats approaching the cove as he raced through the gap in the massive slabs of rock. The two dolphins, Dee and Slate, hovered in the clear water as he peered into the entrance to the crevice. He pointed to the dark channel and Dee swam several lengths into the cave, then backed out and smiled.

Gabrielle's voice crackled in his ears, "The cigarette boat is approaching the freighter. You may begin the procedure, just make sure that you keep track of the time. We don't want to destroy all that we're trying to save!"

"Right you are," replied Raffe.

He slipped into the shadows slowly, hesitantly, and felt a chill run down his spine. He turned to the two dolphins, sentries hanging in the water guarding the entry, and swam into the dark hole. His *orb* glistened like a brilliant red flare scattering across the dark edges in the tunnel like spider webs until he came to the cavern with the blue crystal glowing in the darkness.

The last few days merged into a dizzying blur of lessons, most of which touched on questions that haunted him for years and he had just barely peeked into a jewel box of mysteries. At the same time, his introduction to the underworld spawned a hunger for a complete understanding of the powers that somehow allowed unimaginable dreams of children to be real. Adrian and Mary were amazing but Dadeus and Ponte were fascinating.

He was just beginning to understand the process of reading from the Book of Natural Balance and felt that it was merely the introduction to a trove of eternal wisdoms. Desperate to understand the book itself and, eventually, the physical workings of The Crystals, he felt that the secrets of these powers, developed through thousands of years, were guarded by the moving figures. Raffe floated for a moment to ponder the realization that The Book of Natural Balance was the history of his ancestors.

"Adrian and Mary are descendants of those same people. If Adrian can step inside that giant Red Crystal, I can do this!"

Concentrating on the task at hand, he inserted Adrian's key into the slot in the rock and pressed the amber crystals in order, north, south, east, and west. The Blue Crystal rose up in its mount, shimmering in the darkness. He pulled a large golden crystal, extracted from one of Ponte's instruments, from the pouch on his right arm and exchanged the gems. Placing the Blue Crystal into the bag, he pushed the amber crystals in reverse order. The Golden Crystal descended into the rock.

His headset suddenly crackled with the loud static of white noise. He tapped the earphones through his headpiece but the hiss persisted. He punched the buttons of the tab of his sleeve. *"Too bad there isn't a volume control,"* he thought, *"must be the change in the power. I sure hope Dadeus and Ponte find a way to fix it soon or I'll be crazier than I already am."*

Raffe checked his watch, fifty-eight minutes to go. He shuddered in the cold water and tried to keep his body moving in the cramped space.

"The Crystals have been exchanged," he said into the microphone in his mouthpiece. There was no response, just static rasping through his headset. He shined the *orb* around the dark cave, relieved to see faint blue light seeping through the tunnel from the entrance, and wished that he could escape the cold dark cavern. He tried to breathe slowly, to maintain his center by staring at the glow of the golden crystal, but he could feel the walls closing in around him and the narrow tunnel growing smaller.

Adrian, dressed in his gray diving suit and helmet, remained out of sight as the ghost children and animals herded the pirates through the narrow canyons and up the long crag to the cliffs above the cove. The children spent two days preparing for the campaign and everything was in place. Gray clouds billowed over the plaza, as the children and animals took turns dousing each other with ashes from the fire pit, wallowing in the hollow until they were all the same shade of gray.

The young *seer* had been communicating with Dadeus and Ponte for the past hour. "We have the pirates moving towards the cliff above the cove. We should be there in less than twenty minutes."

"We understand. Raffe's about to install the Golden Crystal…" suddenly, Dadeus' voice disappeared and was replaced by static.

"Hello, hello!" There was no response.

Dadeus and Ponte shut down the power to the underworld and switched on the new circuitry to the transporter. They jumped at the crackling clatter from the speaker, killed the volume, and turned back to their work.

"We've lost communications. We'll just have to hope that everything continues as planned on the surface," said Dadeus quietly. "I hope we've set this up properly. I'll worry about the children until we're finished with this phase of the operation."

"I've faith in Adrian and Raffe," replied Ponte. "They know what they're doing and Adrian has been through two campaigns like this before. He saved the island and then he saved my wife!"

The two men stared at each other, for the briefest moment, before flipping switches and turning dials to precipitate a synthetic storm around the Dragon Queen.

"I wish we could watch the expressions on their faces as the ship is swallowed up by the vortex," smiled Ponte.

"I just wish they could comprehend that what they are about to experience is as close to justice for the children of the island as we can muster. I've watched them leave countless children on the beach over the years and I'm sure they killed the parents. I feel no pity for these pirates. It is their due," said Dadeus without sympathy.

"Were you one of those children?"

"Yes."

Mary stepped forward and placed her hands on Dadeus' shoulders and then planted a kiss on top of his shiny baldhead.

Jorge slowed the Tigger2, as they glided alongside the rusting freighter and Jake threw a line to a crewman standing on the deck. They tied off the sleek craft next to a rusty ladder clinging to the side of the freighter.

"Nice ship!" said Jake sarcastically.

"It has to be non-descript, like a faceless person in a crowd," replied Jorge.

They climbed the ladder and found Edward Li waiting on deck in a white silk suit. He smiled and shook hands with the two men,

"Welcome to the Dragon Queen! She doesn't look like much from the outside but she has the finest engines in the world and the accommodations will surprise you! Please come with me."

He led Jake and Jorge, past a helicopter lashed to the deck, through a lock, and down a flight of stairs. After several turns, he opened a plain steel door to reveal a salon as beautifully decorated as any on the world's finest yachts. Fine leather chairs surrounded a huge teak table, inlaid with gold and stones scribing a fire-breathing dragon. A well stocked bar opened on one side of the cabin flanked by shelves displaying ancient bonsai trees struggling from simple stone trays and orchids, their vibrant flowers floating like butterflies. The walls and cabinetry were constructed of the finest woods and the fabrics and carpeting had been purchased from the most exclusive decorator in Hong Kong. Soft pools of light focused on several massive impressionist paintings hanging on the walls of the cabin.

"May I offer you a drink?" inquired Edward Li.

"Scotch, single malt," replied Jake. "I'm impressed with the accommodations of your ship. It's a silk purse inside a sow's ear!"

Edward poured two fingers into three glasses and passed them to his partners. They toasted and Edward proceeded into the next cabin, "Thank you. I had the guidance of Marcel Ardenoff, who has offices in Hong Kong and Paris. The man is a genius. The result is very comfortable and it certainly serves my purposes."

He stepped through a door into a passage lined with communications gear. A Chinese woman, standing over a console, smiled as Edward waved his hand at the equipment, "This is my assistant, Michelle. We can jam the Coast Guard's radio and radar transmissions and we know where they're patrolling. This provides a certain…security."

Michelle followed the men into the next cabin and gestured for Jorge and Jake to sit on a leather sofa that curved around a long glass table. She brought a silver tray with several small bags of white powder and placed it before Jake, who was mesmerized by her yellow eyes and a mane of dark hair framing an exquisite face, "Thank you."

Michelle cocked her head and smiled. She was wearing an emerald green silk suit that shimmered as she walked behind Edward's chair.

Jake withdrew a small chemical testing kit from his jacket, picked a bag at random, took a small sample on a lance, and added it to a vial. He swirled the mixture around and smiled, "This is very pure. Is it all like this?"

Edward Li smiled and responded, "Yes, it is."

He repeated the test on two more bags, "I'm satisfied. Let's begin the transfer. We'll call the other boats to start the first run."

As the Chinese man raised his glass to toast, the freighter heaved to starboard and then righted itself as a loud clap of thunder echoed through the compartment. Michelle followed the three men as they scrambled out of the cabin and up the stairs to the deck.

Huge thunderheads surrounded the ship, lightning crackled across the sky, and torrents of rain fell about the ship but not a single drop wet the decks.

"What's happening?" screamed Jake.

"I don't know," replied Edward, as he scanned the sky. "The radar shows only clear weather!"

Jorge grabbed a handrail, as the bow of the ship began to descend into the sea. Jake reached out to grab Michelle as she started sliding, gathered her up, and clamored to the stern, as the freighter slipped beneath the surface of the water.

Slowly, the rain and lightning faded away and the skies cleared, leaving no trace of the Dragon Queen or those aboard her.

Adrian walked along just beneath the far side of the ridge, where he could remain unseen and called to Todd and Morgan, his voice muffled by the suit, "We've lost communications with the underworld...so, we're on our own. Let's keep these guys moving and we'll stick with our plan." He held his finger up to his mask to indicate that Todd should not respond. Todd nodded and turned back to roaring at the pirates.

Brandy, the other dogs, fox, wild boar, and several wolves charged down the opposite hill and chased the pirates through the gully, barking and snarling. Directed by Magnus and a swarm of birds, the first group of animals and children rotated into positions along the ridgelines so, wherever the pirates looked for escape, they were surrounded. There was only one path they could follow.

Thimble stumbled and fell into Bernie, "I wish we had our weapons!"

Bernie turned and pushed Thimble back a step, "You can't kill ghosts. They're already dead!"

"I hope this trail leads to the cove and the boats!"

"Run, you fool!"

The pirates tore through the underbrush, dodging snakes that rose up, hissing and pretending to strike. Mice and rats scurried across the path and between their legs. Lions and tigers roared. Wild boar ran up and down the sides of the little valley behind them and just out of reach.

The pirates were herded up a long steep rocky plume until they were perched precariously on the cliffs overlooking the cove as the ghost children and the gray animals converged into a screaming mob and charged up the hill to surround them. Bernie and Thimble turned in panic, leapt into the water beside the idling boats, and clambered aboard. Thimble reached for an automatic pistol, lying on the seat at the rear of the boat, and took aim at the children on the cliff but Bernie snatched the gun and smacked his hand. "We don't shoot children...even if they are ghosts. It's a sacred oath."

The children and the animals peered down on the pirates with a deafening roar. Adrian pushed through the crowd to shine a powerful *orb* down on the men. The pirates shielded their eyes as he focused the lamp, bright as sunlight.

Little Kelly stepped to the front, her blond hair flaming around her silhouette in the brilliance of Dadeus' *orb*, and all of the other children and the animals grew quiet. The cove was almost completely contained by flat rock and her little voice sounded very loud. "We are the ghost children. You have kidnapped countless innocent children over the years and abandoned them on this island to perish. This is our savior. He's come from far away to right the wrongs that you've inflicted on us. He is one of many who will be waiting for you if you ever return to this island."

Adrian turned the *orb* close to the diving suit, which glittered like stardust.

Kelly continued, "Your mother ship is gone. If you don't believe me, call them on your radios!"

Bernie reached for the walkie-talkie and shouted, "Jorge, Jorge, speak to me."

There was no response. He dropped the radio and stared up at the children and animals lining the cliff.

"You'll leave this island and never return. Tell your people that pirating will not be tolerated in these waters or anywhere along the coast. The aliens and the ghost children can make you and your boats disappear at will! This is the Bermuda Triangle of the Pacific. If you want to see tomorrow, you'll leave now!"

The children and the animals roared. The men in the boats fired up their engines and the three speedboats got tangled and mangled as they raced to the entrance of the cove.

Kelly turned to Adrian with her biggest smile. "How'd I do?"

Adrian reached down and gave her a big hug. "You were wonderful," he said through his mask. His voice was muffled but Kelly understood every word.

Raffe was cold and shivering, struggling to contain his claustrophobia and anxious to get back to open water. He checked his watch. *"I sure hope that everything went according to plan. It's time to replace the Golden Crystal."* He pushed the amber crystals in order and the Golden Crystal rose up in its mount.

Suddenly, he sensed movement behind him and spun around to rows of triangular teeth lining the open mouth of a very large shark, who wandered into the tunnel for a protected snooze. The shark did not look happy.

He shined the *orb* in its face, so close that he could see the pupils in the cold eyes constrict, sizing him up, and he knew there was no defense if the shark decided to charge. He had no weapon.

He took a deep breath and turned around very slowly. His whole body trembling, *"I have to replace the Crystal."* He pulled the Golden Crystal from its setting. His hands were shaking so violently that he fumbled and watched the giant gem tumble to the floor of the cave. *"I have to concentrate."* He was breathing very fast and found himself bobbing up and down. He tried long slow breaths but it was no use, so he pulled the Blue Crystal from the pouch on his arm and, using both hands, jammed it into the mount. He was too frightened to turn around and he expected the shark to take a bite out of his back at any moment.

West, East, South, North...The Blue Crystal descended into the rock and began to glow. He pulled the key from the slot and turned back to the shark, pressing his body against the wall of the cave. He closed his eyes and yelled, "Shark!"

An hour of static in Adrian's headset provided a pounding headache. Occasionally, he could hear individual words but he couldn't make out who was talking or what they were saying. Suddenly the static cleared and one word filled his earphones, "Shark!"

He jumped off the cliff and dove through the wakes of the cigarette boats, charging through the cleavage in the rocks to the sea, the air bubble encased his body, and he sped through the cove, diving to depth to find the entrance to the cave.

Dee and Slate were swimming back and forth in front of the dark hole and, if a human could understand the emotions of dolphins, this was panic.

He swam directly into the hole and down into the darkness where he found the tail of a stout white shark. It was so broad that it filled the tunnel. The great tailfin swooshed back and forth in quick agitated thrusts, as if it was unsure about whether to move forward or to back out of the cave.

Instinctively, he grabbed the tail and pulled with all his might. The shark writhed back and forth, bashing him from one wall to the other. The air bubble barely cushioned him and he knew that he couldn't hold on for very long. He pushed his feet into a crevice on his right and pulled. Inch by inch, he struggled to haul the huge monster out of the hole. In frustration, the shark wiggled out backwards with Adrian clinging to its thrashing tail.

As soon as the young *seer* cleared the entrance, he released his grip and dove for the bottom. Dee and Slate moved in to batter the shark with blows from either side before it was fully out of the hole. The shark turned to attack Slate but the dolphin was too quick and dodged the rows of shiny white teeth glistening in its snarling mouth. Dee hammered the shark from the other flank.

Adrian curled up in the rocks on the bottom of the little bay in terror, as the two dolphins drove the shark away from the entrance. He raced back into the crevice to find Raffe at the far end of the dark hole, pressed flat against the wall next to the glowing crystal. Adrian swam to him and grabbed his arm. There didn't appear to be any punctures in Raffe's diving suit but he could feel his friend shaking violently. He pealed the golden key from his hand and wrapped an arm around him, "Are you okay?"

"The shark...is it gone?" gasped Raffe.

"Yes, Dee and Slate are taking care of him."

"He was so close that I could have reached out and punched him in the nose! I heard engines in the water. Are the pirates gone?"

"They're gone and they won't be back. Come on let's get you out of here!"

"I dropped the crystal!"

"We'll come back for it! Now go!"

Chapter Twelve

Seaman First Class Billy Dee leaned back into the leather chair staring at his console in the Naval Yard in San Diego. With access to satellite, radar, sonar, and video, he could identify every ship docked in the Naval and commercial harbors and, with input from the rest of the team, account for every craft that was moving within hundreds of miles. With the zoom on the cameras, he could snap portraits of workers, who were supposed to be loading and unloading cargo, hiding behind a row of dumpsters taking a cigarette break.

It had been a slow day. Two frigates docked and a pair of subs and four cruisers set a course southwest to join up with a carrier group. Yachts moved in and out of the private marina, tankers and freighters docked and offloaded their cargoes with precision and speed, and numerous utility craft were moving between ships but everything was normal.

The sailor scanned the screens and took a long slow sip of his coffee to fend off the boredom of the routine. The sun was low on the horizon, scattering golden glitter across the Pacific. Only two hours remained before his shift ended.

He sat bolt upright, roused from the monotony by a large blip on his screen and a squawk from the speaker, "What the…?"

His CO, David Smythe, turned at the outburst, "What do you have?"

Billy Dee stood up, grabbed a pair of binoculars, and peered out the window. He could not believe his radar screens. There, in the middle of the Naval ships, was a large rusty freighter. The name across her stern read Dragon Queen, Hong Kong. It had not been there a moment before…it just bobbed to the surface.

He pointed out the window, "Where'd that come from?"

"Get 'em on the horn and find out! Now!"

Billy grabbed the microphone, "Harbormaster to Dragon Queen, identify yourself and...where did you come from?"

There was no response. He punched a button on the console to call the harbor patrol but two coast guard cutters were already closing on the rusting hulk. Billy could see members of the crew running around the deck of the old ship and there were four people, dressed in civilian clothes, knotted at the stern. Two men ran out of the bridge, jumped into the water, and started swimming towards a dock. Armed guards were waiting for them.

Edward Li, Jorge, Jake, and Michelle huddled together, hugging the rail at the stern of the ship. Michelle grasped Jake's arm like a leach on bare skin and Jorge kept turning around and around in a slow desperate dance, searching for some escape. The ship had been enveloped in a strange silver bubble and moved at an incredible speed under water for hundreds of miles, yet they weren't even wet. The terror of their mysterious journey paled when they realized that the Dragon Queen had surfaced in the middle of a naval yard.

A coast guard cutter approached from starboard and a commanding voice erupted from a speaker, "Show yourselves on deck and be prepared for boarding!" Another cutter was just pulling along the port side and grappling hooks clanged across the decks, snatched onto railings, lines pulled taught by a squad clamoring onto the old freighter.

"I fear that our promising enterprise is to be short-lived, my friends," said Edward Li, as he raised his hands and walked towards the American sailors who were scrambling across the deck like so many ants attacking a picnic basket in the heat of summer.

Adrian and Raffe peaked out of the tunnel. Dee and Slate were hovering in the water just outside the entrance, their snouts bowed in apology before offering triumphant smiles.

Ponte's voice erupted in their earphones, "Well done lads! The freighter is sitting in the Naval yard in San Diego. I'd love to see the expressions on the faces of the harbormaster…and the pirates on that ship!"

The two boys swam from the fissure and zoomed through the water to a beach just north of the cove. The two dolphins rose out of the surf clicking madly, dove below the surface, and jumped into the air.

The ghost children and all of the animals scampered down the cliffs cheering loudly. Adrian and Raffe pulled off their helmets and wrapped each other in a hug. "We've done it. They're gone!" shouted Raffe. "And thanks for saving my butt, I'd sort of accepted that the shark wasn't going to let me out of that cave."

"No problem, this's better than being fish food."

The other children ran up and tackled the two *seers*. All of the animals joined in and the larger animals paraded riders up and down the little beach in a jubilant march. Magnus and a swarm of birds of every variety flew above their heads and laughter and cheers filled the air.

Finally, Raffe whistled and raised his hand, "My friends…both human and animal!"

Everyone laughed together.

"With the help of our new friends from Morgan's Knot, it seems that we've succeeded in our quest. I thank each of you for your help and I think it's time that we washed off the ashes that have provided our security for so many generations for a final time. Everyone in the water!"

The children and animals scrambled down the sand into the surf and washed each other until their normal colors glistened in the warm glow of an orange sun setting in the west, a blazing orb slipping into the deep blue Pacific beneath a splay of streaks fanning out to paint puffy white clouds with yellow and red.

Sara gasped for air when the hologram suddenly flashed to life displaying a swarming herd of children, intermingling with a rather amazing collection of animals, prancing across the beach near the cove in celebration of a revolution. The sound suddenly crackled to life, children cheering and animals making all sorts of animal noises.

At the first image, Sara jumped to her feet and hugged John, George, and Travis. There could be no doubt that Adrian's plan had succeeded and the pirates were gone forever.

The entire population of the underworld rushed through the tunnels to the waterfall on the surface. Adults streamed out of the secret passage behind the cascading water and ran down the path to the plaza, just as the children and the animals returned from the beach.

Parents, separated from their children for years, ran without hesitation and gathered them in their arms. Childless adults embraced children who had been abandoned by the pirates. Gabrielle and Mary found Todd and Sandy and hugged them as they would their own. Every child was matched with adults and no one was left out.

The animals joined in the festivities, nuzzling against the humans who stroked and hugged them in return. Lions and tigers roared, the pack of wild boar snorted loudly, horses whinnied, goats and sheep bayed, and birds sang and flew around the heads of the children. The two giraffes and their young leaned down to lick several bald heads in the pandemonium. Kelly and a few of the youngest climbed into the laps of the bears, who wrapped them in their arms and licked their faces.

Sara ran to Adrian and engulfed him in a hug, "I was so worried about you and now I am so very proud!"

"Raffe did the hard part! A shark almost got him!"

Tic and Brandy wandered up and rubbed against Adrian's legs, "We hear that you saved Raffe from the shark," said Tic.

Brandy smiled, "You're a hero again!"

"I'm no hero. I've just done what had to be done and, once again, I have you two to thank."

Tic sat down and licked his paws, "This is becoming a habit. I'm tired. Can we take a breather now?"

Adrian leaned down and scooped Tic up in his arms, "I hope we're finished with all of this. You said that being a *seer* came at a great price and I had no idea how true that would be."

"You've earned the honor to be called a master *seer* and we're all proud of you. Now, I'm ready to get back to taking naps in the sun in the window at the observatory on Morgan's Knot! Since I met you, I've used up two or three of my nine lives. I need a rest."

Everyone returned through the passage behind the waterfall to the underworld and the children were overwhelmed by the wonders that existed right beneath their feet. They moved from one dome to the next and listened intently to explanations of the technology of the Crystals and the interaction with the sea. The residential dome was already being expanded and accommodations were prepared for every child from the surface.

Ponte and Dadeus finished rewiring the circuits, disrupted by the day's events, and stepped out of the control room onto a catwalk to view throngs of people moving about below.

"Do you realize that this is the first time in our history that the music of young children's voices has resonated in these domes?"

"It is a wonderful sight and one that should never change," smiled Ponte. "This is your beginning. You already control the powers of the Crystals, now you have a complete society to expand on that knowledge."

"I hope we'll find ways to use it wisely."

The two men hugged and walked down the stairs to join the crowd below.

As night crept across the Pacific, a giant bonfire erupted in the center of the plaza. The animals were invited to join the festivities and a feast was served for all. The sky overflowed with stars and a waning moon cast enough light to form faint shadows under the palms and banyans around the square. The scent of wonderful foods and the crackling glow of the fire enhanced an ambiance of hope and relief.

After the feast, Gabrielle stood and raised his hands for silence. A hush crept through the crowd as they turned to face their elder.

"My friends, this is truly a momentous day. For the first time, we are all together and we will never again allow the pirates to dictate our way of life. We'll join the wonders of the underworld with the beauty and bounty of the island to form a perfect balance. I believe we have the children and the animals to thank for our deliverance."

The crowd clapped and cheered.

Gabrielle raised his hands and, again, the crowd grew quiet, "There are several heroes that should be recognized. First, Raffe would you stand and join me?"

Raffe hugged his parents and stood up. Everyone cheered as he made his way to Gabrielle, silhouetted in front of the bonfire. He looked slightly embarrassed and smiled bashfully.

"This young man executed the most crucial task in our plan. In the process, he was threatened by a great white shark but he proceeded with his responsibility without hesitation. That is the mark of a true hero."

There were cheers, clapping, snorts, whinnies, roars, meows, barks, chirps, singing, and every sound that a living creature could make in appreciation.

"I would like to present you with a gift from all of us. In the process of joining the underworld…to which he had not been invited," Gabrielle laughed, "we found that he is a *seer*, a reader of the ancient texts. We thought that we had only one other *seer* in our midst, Mary would you stand?"

Everyone clapped.

"We would like to present you with the Book of Natural Balance. You will, of course, have to share it with Mary as her student but accept this as a symbol of our esteem for you and our hope that you will help to guide us into the future." Mary held out the golden book and Raffe took it in his arms, then turned to face the cheering crowd with a modest bow.

"Next I would like to ask Tic, Brandy, and our splendid eagle, Magnus, to step forward." Tic and Brandy looked at each other and trotted to the front of the crowd. "These animals introduced the children and the animals to the concept of The Balance. It is a way of life that we will follow from this day forward."

"I realize that you do not normally wear collars but we have a very special collar for each of you. Each bears the insignia of the ancient *seers* on a medallion and I hope that they will remind each of you of our appreciation for your contribution to our new world."

Gabrielle and Mary attached the collars around Tic and Brandy's necks and slipped a tiny medallion on a slender chain over Magnus' head. The crowd clapped and cheered and everyone reached to stroke them, as they strolled back to their places with Adrian, George, Ponte, Travis, John, and Sara.

"I've saved the best for last. Adrian would you come forward, please."

The crowd went crazy and the noise was deafening, as Adrian was thrust to the front of the crowd, blushing.

Gabrielle wrapped an arm around the boy's shoulders, "My friends, this young man showed us the way. I have to admit that I was a bit skeptical when all of this started but he not only came up with a strategy but a plan that would allow all of us to be joined together from this day forward. He is to be thanked for his intelligence, his bravery, and his sensitivity to our culture. Without his idea and without his leadership, none of this could ever have happened."

Adrian looked out at the hundreds of people and animals, standing around the plaza, clapping and cheering.

Gabrielle raised his hands, "I would like to present you with this medallion with the symbol of the ancient *seers*. It is a perfect cross, surrounded by the arms of the crescent moon and tended by a tiny star. I hope you will wear it with pride and that it will remind you of our appreciation for the wonderful things that you have done for us. We will be forever in your debt." He reached out and placed the necklace around Adrian's neck.

"Thank you," said Adrian as he looked down at the pendant suspended on a heavy golden chain. The background was deep, vibrant blue and the emblem of the cross and the crescent moon was embossed above the surface of the medallion, shimmering with the iridescence of pearls.

He smiled up at Gabrielle and accepted a giant hug, as the crowd moved forward to embrace him.

After the festivities, everyone returned to the domes for the night. Morgan, Molly, Megan, Kelly, Josh, and Ian joined George, Ponte, and Travis in the guest quarters. Raffe gave Adrian a big hug before he wandered off to his room.

Adrian followed his parents to their small apartment and, before the door closed, his father said, "I don't really know how to express the pride that I feel but I hope you understand how special you are."

Adrian hugged his dad. Sara wrapped her arms around her men, "Let me see your medallion!"

He turned and she lifted the pendant, "Oh, my...! This is familiar, isn't it?"

Adrian flashed on the old man in the market stall in Jamaica, "I forgot to tell you about an old man I met in Jamaica!"

Before he could finish, she interrupted, "...an old black man, with a little white goatee and spectacles on the end of his nose. He talked to me about the ancient people who had come to Jamaica from Central America to escape the invaders and he knew about *seers*!"

"He said that he talked with a beautiful lady with blue eyes like mine and I knew it was you!" said Adrian. "He said he would see me again. Ponte and I wondered how he knew about *seers*."

"I have no idea but, perhaps, we could convince the rest of the crew to pass through Montego Bay on our way back to Morgan's Knot, so we can find out more about the old man and what he knows."

"That does bring us to the question of where we go from here. You were heading for Vancouver. I was left on Morgan's Knot, and we're here on another magical island. Where do we go?"

John had been quiet for a while, watching his son and his wife with a wonder that only a parent can feel, "When I met your mother, I was determined to pursue my goals. I wanted to live and work with my colleagues on or near the sea. I wanted to accomplish things in my life that would have merited little meaning on Morgan's Knot. Your mother was foolish enough to give up her world in exchange for her love for me and I was too blind to see the wonders and the opportunities of life on the islands of the Crystals."

"After all that I've seen here and talking with Ponte, George, and Travis about what's been happening on Morgan's Knot, I've realized that I made a mistake. Our family is a part of the magic of these islands and we should contribute our talents and efforts to The Balance. The question is whether we should stay here or return to your mother's home."

Sara beamed, "I think he's finally got it but it sure took long enough!"

Adrian was suddenly serious, "I love this place and I really want to learn more about diving and the sea, but they have two *seers* here and I think that we ought to go back to Morgan's Knot. It's become home."

Chapter Thirteen

Over the next few days, the island buzzed with activity. Gabrielle and Mary guided Adrian and Raffe through a series of tunnels into the pyramid. The channel opened into a giant room, above the chamber of the Red Crystal, illuminated by shafts of sunlight streaming through the slits that the children found in the cap.

The walls were covered with the familiar figures that bore the secrets in the Book of Wisdoms and the Book of Natural Balance. Mary guided the boys to a panel that illustrated the beginning of the story.

It displayed the history of an ancient society rich in knowledge, far ahead of the technology of the time, and balanced with the world around the island of Atlantis. "They were a people who enjoyed great wealth through trade with civilizations that were emerging on all of the continents and they shared their knowledge through those contacts."

"Their society deemed men and women equals, the fertility of women was worshipped, and children were gifts from the Gods. Everyone received an education in the powers of The Crystals, the wonders of the natural world, and the concept and practice of The Balance."

"Medicine was far more advanced than in any other part of the planet and their ships always returned with medicinal plants and treatments they found through their trading partners. The people of Atlantis created a sophisticated society that merged the needs of humans with the magic of the animal world and, in many ways, it was far more advanced than the world we live in today…and they were not the only progressive civilization centered around and powered by the Crystals. They were the first to successfully chronicle their world in the texts but their chapter closed with a cataclysmic explosion that incinerated the island and dispersed the few ships that escaped to carry the secrets across the world."

The next panel presented the tale of Protus and the survivors aboard Jofre's ship sharing their knowledge of the magic with the local peoples in Central America. The concept of The Balance spread across the land and eventually spawned the germination of rich cultures that swelled across the Central Americas. The next frame showed the European invasion that conquered, pillaged, and destroyed cultures and societies born through centuries of refinement. Just as Morgan gathered those original families and sailed to Morgan's Knot, these illustrations told of Safra, Ameridus, and Nanu assembling their people and the sacred texts to begin their journey to Jamaica and then the Island of the Children.

"They named the island with the hope that it might become the reincarnation of their home in the tradition of Atlantis. Their ships ferried the white stones from a quarry on the mainland to build the ancient city and their society flourished for hundreds of years, until a great battle with the pirates forced a retreat into the volcanic caverns that became the underworld. The pirates destroyed the city and used the island as a protected haven to bury treasures and dispose of the children."

Adrian turned to Mary, "So you are direct descendants of Protus?"

"Yes, we are and now we have the opportunity to finish the work of our ancestors."

"You'll succeed."

"I hope you're right."

They moved to final panel, a distorted map of the world. Gemstones were inlaid in, what is now, Egypt, Israel, Rome, England, China, the Andes, and one on the east coast of the United States. Mary pointed, "No one's ever deciphered the meaning of this one. It's a complete mystery."

"Maybe it's something that's going to happen," suggested Raffe.

"That's as good a guess as anyone else has come up with, so perhaps we'll find out one day. In the meantime, Gabrielle and I have decided to use this space as a school for the children. We couldn't think of a more appropriate place to pass this knowledge from one generation to the next."

"What a wonderful idea! No one could ask for more inspiration."

Raffe turned from the last panel. "So, like you, I am descended from these people. I can almost feel the weight of their hopes and dreams and I can't wait to begin."

Mary wrapped an arm around his shoulders, "I think that we'll succeed over time, especially with students like you!"

"Perhaps we should return to the others. There's much to do."

Ponte and Dadeus remained cloistered for days, working with the circuits and the vectors. Communications between the island and Ester, Alius, Jofre, Nanchez, and Mandor on Morgan's Knot initiated the process of establishing secure accounts to receive covert shipments of rubies produced by the island's giant Crystal. With the resulting funds, they could import tools and materials to begin construction on the surface.

The children of Morgan's Knot led George and several of the men of La Isla de los Ninos to the growing fields along slender plateaus at the south end of the island. George confirmed their theory that these meadows had once been used for growing crops before the descendants of Nanu and Protus were driven underground. The vectors were strong, the soil was fertile, and the water flowing up through the rocks was pure and clean. On further exploration, they found orange and lemon trees, corn, sugarcane, cotton, and several varieties of squash growing wild on level fields that had been carved along either side of the ridge.

Travis and John worked with the Soule and Amy to develop a strategy for trading with the villages and cities along the coast. Their first task was to move the ships, anchored in the interface, to the cove, where they could be readied.

Sara, Mary, and Gabrielle created a basic curriculum for the new school and carpenters were busy building chairs and desks in the cavernous space inside the pyramid. Vectors were set up to project holograms and wiring installed for videos and the Internet.

Tailors worked night and day to produce diving suits for the children and classes were organized to introduce the underworld's newest inhabitants to the wonders of the sea.

The children from Morgan's Knot were the first to be scanned and outfitted in the gray suits and the tailors labored to incorporate all the systems into a suit small enough for little Kelly.

Soule and Amy instructed the group on the properties of the diving suits and the basics of moving through the water.

Adrian joined his friends and paired up with Kelly, "You're going to love this!"

"I'm a little bit scared. I know how to swim but I've never been under the water except when I'm riding Spot or Dusty."

"Just breathe normally and you'll be fine. The first time they took me out, I was breathing really fast and kept bobbing up and down. Just stay beside me and I'll make sure that you're okay."

Kelly smiled and pulled the little helmet over her head. Her voice crackled in Adrian's headset as he secured the seal, "Do I look like an alien?"

The *seer* laughed, "The world's smallest alien!"

They walked, glove in glove, down the ramp into the water and swam slowly through the dome into the open sea. The bubbles formed around each of the divers, stretching out as they moved through the glistening wonderland. Jagged rays of golden sunlight skittered down through the water and schools of brilliantly colored fish darted away from the swimmers as they gained speed.

"Now, just breathe normally and move your arms to your sides. You'll gain speed. When you want to slow down, push your arms out. Turn your body in the direction that you want to move. It's just like riding a wave on the surface."

Kelly giggled, pulled her arms to her sides, and zoomed ahead. "Like this?"

"I think you've got the right idea…slow down, wait for me!"

Soule and Amy guided the group to a long reef that blossomed from white sand on the bottom, the corrals providing a living, breathing home for an incredible variety of fish. Schools of fairy basslets tumbled like orange and pink clouds and a swarm of yellow tang darted around the children, nipping at the glistening bubbles clinging to their diving suits, curious about the new small visitors. Giant grouper cruised slowly along the bottom and a shiny silver mangrove snapper passed above them. Tiny fish flitted and shrimp hovered in the cover of the fans and grasses, in an attempt to escape a brilliant red coral hawkfish nipping in and out of the corrals searching for a meal.

Amy's voice crackled through the headsets. "This is a world to observe but don't touch anything unless you know what it is. Some of these creatures aren't particularly friendly. Remember, we really are aliens invading their world, so let's show some respect."

Molly and Megan were racing along the bottom, laughing and giggling at the freedom and speed of their movements. Their bubbles glittered in brilliant shafts of light cascading down from the surface. Josh and Ian swept through sea grasses waving like wheat in the fields at home. Several blue spotted rays rose up from the sand to greet them and rolled over into back flips that rocked the headsets with giggles and laughter.

Lobster, crab, and urchins patrolled along the bottom and several sand sharks darted in curious circles around the children. Barracuda flashed like shifty silver beacons, twisting into abrupt turns to catch a convenient victim. Dee and Slate swam up to the group and bumped Adrian with a gentle nudge. They were both smiling and zoomed along with the children as they explored the reef.

Morgan swam over to Adrian and Kelly, "This is truly magical. I wish we could take these suits home with us!"

"We'll have to ask Soule and Amy whether that might be possible. Even though the people on Morgan's Knot are in balance with the creatures of the sea, I guarantee they've never enjoyed an experience like this!"

Kelly swam into a swarm of blue and yellow butterfly fish that were spinning around in a glistening ball. She pushed her hand into the middle of the sphere and the little fish enveloped her arm. "If I wasn't wearing this suit, I bet they would tickle!"

The divers continued along the reef and every child dove down to explore each new wonder. Amy's voice interrupted the laughter, "Here's something that we don't get to see very often." She pointed up to a huge gray mass that breached the surface and dove along the reef.

Kelly shrieked, "What's that?"

Amy laughed, "It's a whale shark. It's looking for plankton and tiny shrimp. The water is rich with life at the moment because the currents are cold and full of nutrients. It's one of the most gentle creatures in the ocean, even if it is related to the sharks.

The giant fish cruised through the ocean with long, loping swings of an endless tail, its mouth open, a giant sieve straining nourishment from the sea. The jaws were large enough for a grown man to stand upright inside. Swarms of smaller fish followed close to the gaping jaws, feeding on scraps and leftovers, and pilot fish clung just beneath its stomach, riding the wave created in its slow graceful movement. The huge body blocked the sunlight, like a giant storm cloud, and slowly disappeared from view.

"That's fantastic," laughed Molly. "It's bigger than a bus!"

"They're one of the wonders of the sea," said Amy. "We only see them once or twice a year, as they follow the blooms of plankton. I always wonder how far they travel to complete their circuit from the far north to the below the equator. It must be thousands of miles!"

Finally, Soule's voice crackled over the headsets. "We've been down here for quite a while and it's time to head back to the dome. Let's race!"

With that challenge, all of the children gathered around Soule and Amy and zoomed through the water back to the island. Dee and

Slate peeled off from the group with a wave of their tails and loud, rapid clicking, as the divers approached the interface.

They padded up the incline inside the dome and Morgan pulled off her helmet. She wrapped along arm around Adrian, "That's so much fun and the reef and the fish are so beautiful. We have to take this technology back with us."

Molly and Megan were bubbling with excitement, "That's about as close to flying as a human can get. We're ready to go again!"

Josh and Ian pulled off their helmets, "Thanks for taking us! That was wonderful. Will we get another chance before we have to leave?"

"We hope that you'll all join us each day for a class until you start your journey home. There's much more that we'd like to teach you. We'll meet you here tomorrow morning."

Kelly hugged Amy, "I think I want to be a fish when I grow up!"

"I know just how you feel. I've been diving for years and I still feel that same excitement every time we swim out of this dome."

Morgan stepped up to ask, "Do you think that we could take this technology back to Morgan's Knot? I know our people would benefit from all that you've learned."

Amy smiled, "These suits are custom fitted for each diver, so I don't see any problem with all of you taking them home with you. I know that Ponte and Dadeus are trading secrets, so it wouldn't surprise me to find a facility like this on Morgan's Knot someday."

Morgan beamed, "Oh, thank you. We'll put them to good use!"

The children changed out of their diving suits behind the frosted doors and moved through the tunnels to meet Raffe, who was spending several hours each morning studying the Book of Natural Balance with Mary. They volunteered to teach the other children about the wonders of The Balance.

The animals led the children through the jungle to their lairs and nests and converged on the plaza each evening. For the first time, the children began to help adult animals care for their young.

Molly and Megan showed the other children how to milk a goat and a cow and Josh and Morgan taught them how to collect honey without destroying the hives of the bees. Sheep were shorn and the carpenters provided spinners to transform the wool into yarn. The animals showed the children the plants they used as medicine and samples were collected for the doctors and technicians in the labs in the underworld.

Each evening, all of the children gathered around a bonfire in the plaza to listen to the stories of the history of the Crystals and the island. The elders wanted their knowledge of life on the surface to be integrated into the plans that were being formulated for the future of the island.

Adrian was asked to relate the knowledge that he had collected during his visits inside The Crystals. He used the giant storm on Morgan's Knot to illustrate that the third Crystal provided stability.

He ended his story by saying, "I'm new to this way of life. I was raised, just like some of you, in the normal world and I had no idea that I was a *seer*. I would never have understood the balance that can and should exist between man and nature everywhere but I know I'll dedicate my life to preserving and expanding everything we believe in. I ask you to do the same. It's our responsibility to maintain and protect the powers of the Crystals. Use them wisely and find new ways to expand our knowledge. The future of The Balance will be in your hands."

"We'll be leaving your island and we'll take many of the things that we've learned back to Morgan's Knot. I hope we leave you with an understanding of what the world should be. If there are two islands like this, then there are probably others and the world would be a better place if we could find a way to join together all of the people who inhabit these magical places and all of the knowledge that they've developed over the centuries."

Over the next days, most of the adults and children from Morgan's Knot became proficient in accomplishing tasks in the ocean.

Travis and Ponte spent a great deal of time learning how the sea people used the vectors to control the weather, move large objects around under water, tap the power of the Crystals to transform sea water into fresh, and understand a far more sophisticated system to transform the vector network into sonar and radar than Ponte's primitive barrier on Morgan's Knot. George, Sara, and John studied the processes of growing and harvesting the plants of the ocean for food and medicines, and everyone learned the basics of underwater construction to help in the assembly of the new wing that was being added to the residential dome.

On the last day, George called the group together, "I've decided to stay for a while longer. We're beginning to clear the fields along the ridgeline for crops and I'd like to stay long enough for our friends to begin the first growing cycle. I've talked with Elsie and she's reluctantly agreed to let me stay for a few more weeks. I'd also like to help set up their accounts on the mainland. Much as I'd prefer to accompany you on your voyage, I'll have to take a flight and, who knows, I might get back before you do."

"The children are well schooled in the mechanics of the Jasmine and they've all become experts in navigation, so the adults should be in good hands!" said Travis.

Everyone laughed.

The entire population of the island gathered around the cove to share hugs and thanks, as the group boarded the Jasmine. The animals, lining the cliffs above, roared as Brandy and Tic perched on the foredeck wagging their tails.

Raffe found Adrian and wrapped him in a bear hug, "I know I've a lot to learn about being a *seer* but you set an example that I'll strive to imitate."

"You'll make a fine *seer*. Just remember what Tic told me, that the responsibility of being a *seer* is demanding. It is up to us to defend The Balance."

"I'll do my best and we'll be in touch through the vectors when you get back."

Gabrielle and Mary moved to the front of the crowd and found Adrian before he stepped aboard the Jasmine, "We've you to thank for returning our children and showing us the power of the Balance. I see that you're wearing your medallion and I hope you'll carry it with pride. You've earned our respect and our gratitude."

Adrian looked down at the blue and white pendant, "It's the responsibility of a *seer* to protect and expand the powers of the Balance. I did what needed to be done, nothing more."

Gabrielle smiled down at Adrian, as he raised his hands, and a hush rolled across the smiling faces that were gathered around the cove.

"My friends, there is no way to adequately express our appreciation for all that you have done for us. You chased away dark clouds that have been hanging over our island for centuries and you showed us the life that should exist in this wondrous place. The stories of your contributions will join those on the walls beneath the pyramid as a lasting history. We are in your debt and we hope that The Balance that exists on La Isla de Los Ninos and Morgan's Knot will be joined forever. Have a safe journey."

Travis started the old engines and slowly turned the Jasmine around to the mouth of the cove. Dee and Slate swam ahead of the old boat and leaped into the air as Magnus circled above. Everyone waved and cheered as the trawler disappeared through the crevice in the rocks and headed south.

Adrian wore his real clothes for the first time since he and Raffe descended into the pit. He put his hand in his pocket and felt the locket that they found on the beach. His mother was standing at the bow and he walked over to lean against her.

"I think you lost something."

"I don't know what, I got you back," laughed Sara.

Adrian pulled the locket and chain from his pocket and put it around her neck.

She smiled, opening the locket and staring at the picture inside, "I'd forgotten about this, so much has happened. Thank you for returning it to me. I love it almost as much as I love you, but you're not the boy you were when this picture was made."

Chapter Fourteen

It was a hot and humid evening and seagulls flitted hopefully around the stern as the Jasmine pulled into the docks in Montego Bay. Sammy, the dockhand, was standing on the end of the pier anticipating their arrival.

"Ah, it's good to see that you've had a safe journey. Welcome back to Jamaica!"

Ian and Megan pushed the bumpers over the starboard gunwale and Josh and Molly tossed lines to Sammy, who tied them off to cleats on the gangway, as Morgan killed the engines. Adrian and Ian helped Sara onto the dock and then lifted Kelly into her arms. John and Travis heaved Ponte's hefty frame onto the wharf and hopped up to talk with Sammy about filling the tanks with fuel and water.

Towels and clean clothes were passed from the boat to the quay, as the crew took turns running to the showers. Adrian was coiling a rope at the stern and Sammy noticed the medallion swinging from Adrian's neck.

He dragged a long hose from the gas pump, knelt down to remove the cap from the tanks, and inserted the nozzle, "That is the sign of the *seer*, Mon. Are you a *seer*?"

"I believe I am," said Adrian quietly, still unsure about how Sammy might know about *seers*.

Sammy held up the ring on his hand with a perfect cross and the crescent moon, "I have no training but I am told that the gift of the *seer* is passed through my family. Will you be seeing Simian in the market?"

"Are you talking about the old man with the little goatee and the tiny glasses in the fabric stall?"

"Aye, that is he. He asked me about you, the last time you were here."

"How did he know I was a *seer* or that I might have met you?"

"He's my uncle and he's the master *seer* on this island. Many people think he's just a crazy old man and perhaps that's just as well."

"I wondered about him."

"He'll be expecting you tomorrow in the market. I'm sure he already knows that you have arrived but I'll tell him tonight."

"How would he know?" asked Adrian.

"I might know the answer to your question, if I was a trained *seer* but I am not. I just know that he knows everything."

After breakfast the next morning, the entire crew marched through the streets to the market. The children, overcome by sights, sounds, and smells, fanned out to explore the stalls. Travis and John trod the center of the lane as children darted this way and that, returning to chatter excitedly about their discoveries.

Adrian, Ponte, and Sara walked directly to the fabric stall and Adrian turned to his mother and Ponte, "I'd like to talk with him alone for a moment, if that's alright with you. Sort of one *seer* to another."

They both nodded and wandered over to the trinket stall across the way. Adrian walked up to the old man, who looked up, staring at the medallion hanging on a slender chain from Adrian's neck. He held up his pendant, a perfect match.

"Where did you get that?" asked the old *seer*.

"It was given to me for my service to a group of people who believe in The Balance."

"Ah, The Balance. It is a magical force. I would assume that you are a *seer*. Would that be true?"

"Yes, it would," said Adrian quietly.

"I suspected that you understood the power, the last time we met. Do you remember what I said?"

"Yes, sir. You said that we would meet again."

"And here we are!" laughed the old man. His smile was genuine and his spirit infectious, "Step over here for a moment, there is much that I would like to ask you."

Adrian followed the old man into a shelter of several old timbers covered with a large tattered tarp. Simian put his hand on Adrian's shoulder and his eyes twinkled with delight. Adrian saw a flash and then darkness broken by streaming colors flowing past at an incredible speed. He wondered whether the cosmic kaleidoscope was still and he was moving or visa versa or both and he certainly had no sense of direction or distance. From the moment they flew into the rainbow, he realized that his perception of reality was being remolded into the stuff of children's fantasy or science fiction. In spite of overwhelming terror, he could not conceal his glee.

The history books had, indeed, neglected to include any mention of the shadow world of the powers and the science texts never mentioned the Crystals or the vectors. Every teacher in the world was guiding their students into ignorance by the simple omission of the most powerful energy source on the planet and the people who mastered the magic.

Sara and Ponte emerged from the trinket stall and looked across the way. Adrian and the old man had vanished.

They gathered Travis, John, and the other children, and scoured the market. There was no trace of Adrian or the old man. After more than an hour, they retraced their steps to the dock, where they found little Sammy who was busy with chores around the wharf.

Travis marched up to the black boy, grabbed him by the arm, and demanded, "Your uncle disappeared with Adrian! What do you know of it?"

"Ah, Mon. Don't worry, he is in good hands," said Sammy with a smile.

Travis noticed the ring on Sammy's hand. "What do you know of *seers?*"

"Simian is a master *seer*. He's spent his life, like a blind man finding his way in a new city, searching to understand the secrets of the ancient texts. I'm sure he just wants to talk with your young man. "

"Where would he have taken him?" inquired Travis, who was not returning the little man's smile.

"Ah, I would guess that they've gone to Dolphin Head. It's just down the coast and it is the biggest mountain on this end of the island. I could show you the way."

"That you will, my young friend. Climb aboard!" He released his grip on the boy's arm and lifted him onto the deck of the Jasmine. Josh and Megan untied the lines from the cleats on the dock as the rest of the crew scrambled aboard. Travis cranked up the engines and backed out into open water.

Everyone was discussing every possibility at full throttle until Sara raised her hand for silence. She looked down at the boy, worried and angry, "Where is my son?"

"I told your friend that I believe he is at Dolphin Head, it's just down the coast. We should be there in about an hour."

Morgan looked up, "We could be there in minutes, if you'd let us swim!"

"I've already lost Adrian and I certainly don't want to lose any more of you!"

"We've been trained to use our suits and we know how to take care of ourselves when we have to. You weren't on Morgan's Knot when we rescued Ester but you know what we accomplished on the Island of the Children."

Sara turned to Ponte, flustered, torn by a maternal heart that cherished these youngsters as children while knowing the bravery they contributed to rescuing Ester and chasing the pirates off La Isla de los Ninos.

Ponte smiled. "I think you should allow them to go find their friend. They know what they're doing and I have great respect for their abilities and maturity and admiration for their offer. Besides, Magnus can monitor their progress."

The giant bird squawked, "I'll watch over them."

Sara turned back to Morgan, "I don't like this but I know you're right. Go put on your diving suits."

Travis appeared with the charts and laid them out in front of Sammy, "Show us where they've gone."

Sammy ran his finger west along the northern coast of the island on the map. "They'd be here, Mon," pointing to a small inlet below the mountain, "They call it Dolphin Head. There's a group of thatched villas at the edge of the forest above this little bay. In the center of the largest hut is a stairway that leads down into the chamber where the Crystal turns."

Ponte looked at the boy with a mischievous grin, thinking, *"My instruments were correct, there is a Crystal here!"*

Tic strolled across the table, sat on the chart, and smiled as Sammy reached to pet him. He looked up at Sara and said, "I think you underestimate the talents of these children. They've proven their abilities more than once and they'll find Adrian long before we get there."

Sammy stared bug-eyed at the cat. His mouth was hanging open, "A talking cat?"

The children gathered around the chart and followed Sammy's hand, as he pointed to the spot. One by one, the children leapt over the side of the boat, inflated an elongated bubble of air, and zoomed off to the west. Morgan was the last to leave the ship, "We'll meet you there!"

Magnus spread his enormous wings and lifted off the rail.

"Now that's the way diving should be," cackled Sammy, as he watched them disappear.

Adrian was euphoric but dizzy and it took a moment to clear his head. He had seen a flash and then darkness blazed with streaming lights, as if the old man was zooming through the inside of a prism at the speed of light. He recognized the sensation, the velocity of movement, yet, there was also a sense that he was still and the world was moving past, a bit like flying through the water in his diving suit with much less effort.

They landed softly in a cave before a giant green Crystal, spinning slowly a foot above the floor. Adrian could feel the power flowing from the giant gem. Simian stood next to him with an impish, childish smile, his hand still resting on Adrian's shoulder.

"How did we get here?"

"When the descendants of Protus left this island, they took the texts with them. We have learned many things about the powers of the Crystal, through trial and error, over the generations but I know there is much we do not understand. I'm hoping that you will teach me to master a bit more of it."

"You didn't answer my question."

"Oh, that. We've learned to use the power to transport ourselves from one place to another. There are magic places on the island and, by focusing on those places, I can move from one to another and anyone that I'm touching will travel with me. It does tend to make you a bit fuzzy but I'm an old man and it's much easier than walking."

"You mean you can transport yourselves over distances just by using the power of the Crystal?"

"Of course! It's easy! We've found that the powers extend out from the Crystal like the spokes of a wheel. We just ride the energy," The little man chuckled. His eyes crinkled and twinkled behind his tiny glasses, "You claim to be a *seer* but you do not know of this power?"

"The one thing I've realized about the Crystals is the more you learn, the more you realize you don't know. I think that it is I who should be learning from you!"

"Well then, perhaps we might exchange information. I understand that your parents and your friends are probably worried about you and I promise to return you to them shortly. I guess I should apologize, I just knew that you hold some of the answers we've been seeking for hundreds of years and I was weak enough to seize the moment without asking your permission. I do apologize."

"That's alright," Adrian looked around the cave. The chamber had been chiseled out of dense rock, flat stones lined up like pews in a church, and, in front of the seats, an angular stone carved into what might have been a rough altar. The Crystal cast a gentle green glow that glittered around the cavern. It reminded him of an early morning fog over the bay in front of the little house that he left only months ago, *"That was another lifetime."*

He looked down at the little man, "Where are we?"

"We're under a place we call Dolphin Head. It isn't really a mountain but, in Jamaica, there are only a few places along the coasts that might be considered real mountains, so we call it a mountain. My ancestors have guarded this cave since the princess and her people left. As you can see by the stone alter, some of our ancestors worshipped the Crystal and made offerings to Gods they thought controlled this great power," said Simian pointing to the ancient monument that stood before the Crystal.

"That's exactly wrong," said Adrian. "We call it The Balance or the equilibrium between man and nature. The whole point of these powers is that all the living creatures should live in harmony. We all benefit from sharing our world."

"These ancient rituals haven't been performed in generations, certainly, long before I was born. I think some of my ancestors got confused or desperate." The old man pondered for a moment, "Then there is a Crystal, like this one, in the place that you come from?"

"Actually, I have seen two other Crystals and I believe they're scattered all across the globe. They always come in pairs, one positive and one negative. This is obviously a positive Crystal but it has a mate close by. One balances the other but, in the wrong hands, the negative Crystal offers opportunities for those who would promote that power into the most evil human exploits. I hope that, eventually, we'll find a way to join together with other *seers,* who are using the powers to promote The Balance, to show the rest of the world what might be. There must be people who live with other Crystals, who have built their societies on the concept of The Balance."

"I am aware of another power. I would guess that it is somewhere off the coast of Ocho Rios to the east. The avenue is very powerful and equally dangerous." The little man squinted his eyes, as if he could see the other Crystal. "How do we learn about The Balance?"

"Well, first, we do not slaughter animals for food or clothing. The animals that live on the island that I come from talk with the people. We work together to make the island better for everyone…animal or human, and we respect and value their contributions. There's a dog, a cat, and an eagle on our boat, who've become allies and friends. I couldn't have accomplished the things I have over the past few months without their guidance and assistance."

"I see what you mean. How did you learn to talk with the animals?"

"I honestly don't know the answer to your question. I was totally astonished the first time Tic, the cat, spoke to me. I wasn't born there but my mother was, so there's still a whole bunch that I've yet to learn about the powers of the Crystals and The Balance."

"Your mother was the lady with the beautiful blue eyes?" smiled the old man.

"Yes, I'm sure she's getting a bit anxious about what happened to me," replied Adrian, flashing on the look in his mother's eyes, somewhere between worry and anger, when he attempted something she deemed dangerous and that seemed to be happening a lot lately.

"I understand but answer a few more questions for me before we go."

"Alright," replied Adrian, who was now worried about his parents.

"How did you learn about these things?"

"Well, there was an emergency. There were no living *seers* and I was the only child on the island who hadn't been tested. I had no idea that I had any special gift and certainly didn't think I'd pass the test. Obviously, I was mistaken. I just understood it and found out later that only a true *seer* can understand the texts."

"The Book is called the Book of Wisdoms. It's been handed down from one generation to the next for thousands of years. I'm not sure that it could be copied. It is written in a strange language that makes no sense to anyone but a *seer*. We believe that *scribes* who lived on Atlantis produced these books and many pairs might have escaped an eruption that destroyed the civilization. As you know, the *seer* Protus carried the copy that arrived here. His descendants now live on a small island in the Pacific called La Isla de los Ninos."

"Interesting name, the Island of the Children, because it fulfills the legend," mused the old man. "I have to admit that we are frustrated. We know there is untapped power in this giant Crystal but we have no way of understanding how to use it properly. I believe I am descended from the ancients who discovered this Crystal, several hundred years ago, and my wish is to find and study these texts."

"As a matter of fact, there are two books on the island that I come from. One seems to be guided by the positive crystal and the other by the dark stone. I don't know whether they provide the same information. Perhaps we might share what we know, if we felt that you were truly a *seer* and that you'd use the knowledge to promote and defend The Balance."

"I've spent my entire life trying to grasp this spinning mystery and my ancestors found many things that emanate from this Crystal. We know where the land is extremely fertile, we can follow some of the avenues of power that extend out into the land and the sea, we can move ourselves across those lines, but we do not know how to harness this power to help our people. We can only protect the Crystal from those who might use it for other purposes or, worse, destroy it."

"I understand your frustration but you must understand that these powers have limits. If too much energy is drawn from the Crystals or there is an imbalance, they will cease to exist. That's what happened to Atlantis. Jamaica has a large population. It would be hard to keep this a secret."

"We are a land of many strange beliefs. There are those who believe in Christianity, in Mohammed, in Voodoo, in the visions that they see when they take their drugs, and in the tribal traditions of our heritage...some even talk of returning all of the black people to Africa. There are foreigners who come and buy property to build expensive holiday homes to stay a few months a year, industrialists who ravage the land for bauxite and crops, and the rest scramble to claim a tiny parcel for their own. Underneath all of that, there is a population that struggles to survive. We are a proud and, oddly, happy people. We've protected this secret with our lives for many generations and we will continue with that quest because we believe that the Crystal holds an answer to our prayers."

"I'm not sure that it holds the answer to your prayers but I know that those who believe in the powers of the Crystals are also dedicated to a belief in The Balance. One can not exist without the other."

"I would follow you to wherever, just to learn about these powers. I'm an eager student with no books to work with, teachers to guide me, and no way to transform this power to ease the lives of my people."

"I think the person you need to talk with is my friend, Professor Ponte, the Keeper of the Powers. He'll be fascinated with your ability to transport yourself over the vectors. He's not a *seer* but he's been my guide and knows more than anyone."

"I look forward to meeting him."

"Then perhaps we should get back to my people."

Simian's eyes rolled back in his head, "I don't think we'll have to go anywhere. There are small people coming from the ocean, dressed in very strange costumes...gray with black spots over their eyes."

Adrian laughed, "I know the people you're talking about but how did you know they're coming?"

"Just as we can travel on the avenues of power, we can see along the path. It's like a sixth sense…something that you know, without knowing how you know."

"I have as many questions for you," said Adrian but, before he could ask, the creak of an old door ruptured the rush of air swirling around the cavern. Warm beams of amber *orbs* flashed across the staircase descending from the surface. Six figures in webbed boots clomped down the steps and clustered together at the bottom, their gray suits glistened in the green light sparkling around the cavern, their *orbs* focused on the two *seers* silhouetted in the glow of the Crystal. Adrian's friends braved the unknown to save him and that magic was genuine enough.

Characters – Morgan's Knot

Adrian – son of John and Sara
John – Adrian's father
Sara – Adrian's mother
George – Adrian's uncle on Morgan's Knot
Elsie – Adrian's aunt on Morgan's Knot, Sara's sister
Molly and Megan – George & Elsie's twin daughters
Joshua Keelty – brother of Morgan
Morgan Keelty – sister of Josh
Ian Sheridan – Kelly's brother, Adrian's second cousin
Kelly Sheridan – younger sister of Ian, Adrian's second cousin
Spot and Dusty – dolphins
Professor Ponte – Keeper of the Powers on Morgan's Knot,
astronomer, teacher
Ester – Ponte's wife
Travis – harbor master
Tic – talking black and white tomcat
Brandy – Keelty's Irish setter
Dr. Stevens – doctor on the island
Daphne & Dante – deer, their fowl, Damien
Beggar – small bear
Magnus – large male eagle
Harriet & Harry – hawks
Sammy – Jamaican dockhand, nephew of Simian, student Keeper
Simian –Sammy's uncle, *seer*
Jofre – Master of the *Others* – father of Alius
Mandor – head of production and security
Nanchez – Keeper of the dark powers
Alius – daughter of Jofre – the Other's *seer*, petite
Sheridan – Alius' aunt

Additional Characters – Island of the Children

Roger and Peggy Johnson – owners of the cigarette boat – Tigger 2
Todd & Sandy – son and daughter of the Johnson's
Jasmine – Travis' fishing trawler
Demetre – the Other's harbor master
Yucatan – Mayan characters
       Safra – emperor
       Ameridus – Keeper of the powers
       Thoth – Sun God
       Nanu – Safra's daughter
       Protus – scribe & Nanu's husband
Blackbeard – monkey on the Island of the Children
Raffe – leader of the ghost children
Gabrielle – leader of the Underworld – Mary's husband
Dadeus – Keeper of the Powers for the underworld
Mary – Underworld *seer* – Gabrielle's wife
Jim & Morag – Raffe's parents
Soule & Amy – diving instructors

Edward Li – Chinese drug smuggler
Michelle – Edward Li's assistant
Jorge – Mexican pirate
Jake – drug smuggler
Bernie & Thimble – pirates
Dragon Queen – smuggler's ship
Dee & Slate – dolphins
Seaman First Class Billy Dee – San Diego Naval Yard
David Smythe - Harbor Master – San Diego Naval Yard

The saga continues in

Ice Island

Morgan's Knot - A Serial Fantasy
Episode III

Follow Adrian, Alius, and Raffe as they travel the world to thwart Zepallo, a mysterious villain, who is binding the Dark Crystals into a web of global domination.

Visit www.morgansknot.com

www.ingramcontent.com/pod-product-compliance
Lightning Source LLC
Chambersburg PA
CBHW050742250626
47155CB00005B/1878